Eleanor, Alice, and the Roosevelt Ghosts

Dianne K. Salerni

HOLIDAY HOUSE · NEW YORK

Copyright © 2020 by Dianne K. Salerni

All Rights Reserved

HOLIDAY HOUSE is registered in the U.S. Patent and Trademark Office.

Printed and bound in June 2020 at Maple Press, York, PA, USA.

www.holidayhouse.com

First Edition

1 3 5 7 9 10 8 6 4 2

Library of Congress Cataloging-in-Publication Data

Names: Salerni, Dianne K., author.

Title: Eleanor, Alice, and the Roosevelt ghosts / Dianne K. Salerni.

Description: First edition. | New York : Holiday House, [2020] | Includes
bibliographical references. | Audience: Ages 9–12. | Audience: Grades
4–6. | Summary: "In this alternate version of 1898 New York City,
where ghosts are common household nuisances, young Eleanor and
Alice Roosevelt battle the fierce spirits that are threatening
their family"—Provided by publisher.

Identifiers: LCCN 2019043186 | ISBN 9780823446971 (hardcover)

Subjects: LCSH: Roosevelt, Eleanor, 1884–1962—Childhood and
youth—Juvenile fiction. | Longworth, Alice Roosevelt,
1884–1980—Childhood and youth—Juvenile fiction. | CYAC: Roosevelt,
Eleanor, 1884–1962—Childhood and youth—Fiction. | Longworth, Alice
Roosevelt, 1884–1980—Childhood and youth—Fiction. | Ghosts—Fiction.
Cousins—Fiction. | Roosevelt family—Fiction. | New York
(N.Y.)—History—1865–1898—Fiction.

Classification: LCC PZ7.S152114 Ele 2020 | DDC [Fic]—dc23

LC record available at https://lccn.loc.gov/2019043186

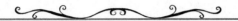

For my siblings and siblings-in-law, who never
fail in their support—

Laurie and Keith

Laura and Brian

Deb and Larry

Three ghastly ghosts erupted in my house

Each one silent and slippery as a mouse.

The Unaware does what it did in life.

The Friendly has fun with its afterlife.

But when I feel that bone-deep chill

I know the Vengeful has come to kill.

A Child's Nursery Rhyme

Author Unknown

~ The Roosevelt Cousins ~

NICHOLAS ROOSEVELT

JOHANNES
JACOBUS
JAMES
CORNELIUS
THEODORE — ❤ — MARTHA BULLOCH

ANNA (BYE) — ❤ — WILLIAM COWLES

THEODORE — ❤ — ALICE LEE

THEODORE — ❤ — EDITH CAROW

CORINNE

ALICE

THEODORE (TEDDY) | KERMIT | ETHEL | ARCHIBALD | QUENTIN

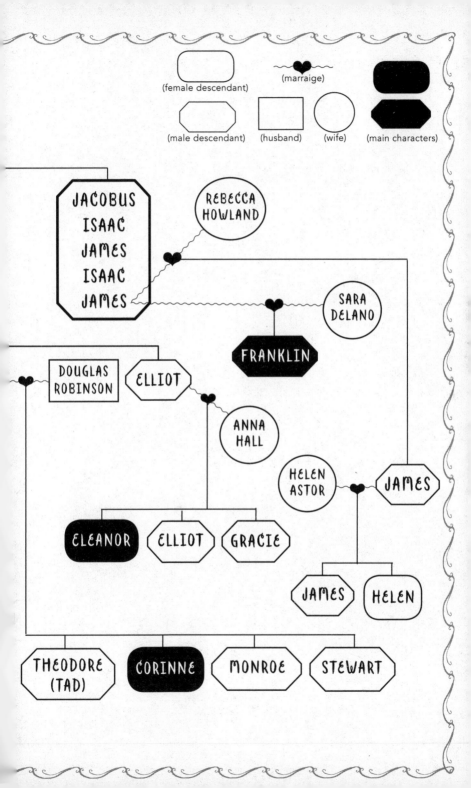

1

ELEANOR DISCONTENTED

ALLENSWOOD. Linden. Wadleigh.

I repeat the names silently, like a prayer, while I wait for Grandmother to finish reading a letter over her afternoon tea. Too nervous to eat a biscuit, I sip from my cup instead and rehearse my approach to a subject that Grandmother no doubt thinks was settled long ago.

Allenswood Academy in London, the school of my dreams.

Linden Hall in Pennsylvania, a perfectly acceptable alternative.

Wadleigh High School for Girls, the one she'll have no reason to say no to.

Nibbling on her tea biscuit, Grandmother turns the sheet of stationery over to the other side, and her eyebrows climb above the rim of her spectacles. Whatever is in this letter, she seems to be devouring it with relish. My grandmother corresponds regularly with elderly ladies up and down the Eastern Seaboard, passing along news of who has died or is likely to die, who is ill, and who has fallen on hard times.

My toe taps a staccato rhythm on the floor while I wait for the right moment to speak. Grandmother's generation doesn't believe in higher education for girls, and she thinks that in my thirteen years I've had all the "book learning" necessary for my station in life. I can argue that public opinion on girls' education is changing, but she'll counter by telling me there is no money for me to attend school, that what little she has is going toward the education of my little brother, Gracie. I have an answer for that.

Across the room, the mantel clock ticks. The wallpaper fades a little bit more. Mice in the walls are born and others die.

Finally, Grandmother lays down the letter and takes off her reading spectacles. "It seems your cousin Alice has been banished from Washington and sent here to New York."

Your cousin Alice. The way someone else might say *Billy the Kid.*

I set down my tea, the last swallow sticking in my throat like a lump of sausage. Another subject of the old ladies' letters is *whose children are behaving badly,* and my first cousin Alice Roosevelt's name has appeared with frightful regularity. "What has she done now?"

"What *hasn't* she done? Chewing gum in public. Breaking curfew. And she's apparently taken up with a gang of boys, riding bicycles, lighting firecrackers under bushes, and I don't know what else!"

"Why is she coming to New York?"

"Your uncle's second wife can't control her. With all the other children that woman has, I suppose she has no time for one that's little more than a wild animal put into good clothes. They're sending her to your aunt Bye in the hope that *she* can stop the girl from running riot."

My shoulders sag. That is what I feared.

"Keep your distance, Eleanor," Grandmother says. "I don't want you picking up any of her unsavory habits."

"I don't think Alice will want to spend time with me." When I last saw Alice, she called me an old stick in the mud because I wouldn't spit off a bridge with her. "But Grandmother, Aunt Bye and I have been working on a quilt for the baby."

Grandmother dismisses our quilt with a wave of her hand. "Let Alice learn to use a needle. Although, if you ask me, it tempts fate to quilt a blanket for a babe one doesn't yet have in one's arms. Especially at Bye's age."

This isn't the first time my grandmother has predicted a tragic end for my aunt's late-in-life marriage and impending motherhood. She revels in the troubles of other people the way a pig wallows in mud, which is an unkind comparison, but I don't feel particularly sorry for it. Especially when she proves me right by taking up another of her favorite topics.

"Truth be told, I would prefer you spend less time in the deathtrap they've made of that house. Electric lights! What newfangled foolishness. Mark my words. Your aunt will be lucky if her entire family doesn't burn up in an electrical fire!"

My shoulders hunch around my ears, even though this isn't the first time she's predicted that fate and probably won't be the last. It's a good time to change the direction of the conversation, and I plunge forward with my planned opening. "Grandmother, did you see the recent editorial in the *Tribune* written by the president of the New York City School Boar—"

The chime of the clock interrupts me, and Grandmother flinches. Shifting in her chair, she squints at the mantel. The dim February sun does little to light the parlor, but Grandmother won't allow the gaslights on until seven, no matter how dark it gets. "Five o'clock already?" My heart sinks when she sets down her teacup, knowing my opportunity has come and gone. "I'm going upstairs to rest before supper, which will be cold meat, served at eight. Tell Rosie."

"I will," I promise, even though supper is always cold meat, served at eight.

Grandmother rises from her chair, as tall and sturdy as a mountain. "I'll see you at supper, then, Eleanor. Return the tray to the kitchen and mind the teacups."

And I always return the tray *and* mind the teacups.

Grandmother hustles from the room, moving faster than one expects from a woman of her age and girth. She wants to be shut in her room by the time her son—my uncle

Valentine—climbs the stairs at precisely sixteen minutes past the hour carrying a shotgun and a bottle of Wild Turkey.

I gather dishes on the tray, and I don't mind the cups as much as I usually do. I'm angry at myself for not addressing the question of my education *before* she opened her mail. The truth is, I dawdled on purpose because . . . until I ask, she cannot say no. If I ask at the wrong time or in the wrong way, I might lose any chance of making my case. Tonight at supper will not be a good time to try again. Grandmother enjoyed her criticism of my Roosevelt relatives far too much to be in the mood to change her mind about anything.

I blame Alice, who will apparently be moving into Aunt Bye's house for the indeterminate future. I imagine her sitting in my favorite yellow chair, taking a needle to the fabric patches *I* cut, and, a few months from now, wrapping the finished quilt around the baby *I* want to cuddle. Why couldn't Alice behave and stay in her own home, where she has a half sister and *four* half brothers of her own, the youngest still a baby himself?

I don't even have Gracie, now that Grandmother has sent him away to school.

It's not that my aunt won't want me visiting while she has Alice to keep her company. Aunt Bye loves a full house and would have hosted all my Roosevelt cousins last Christmas if she hadn't been ill at the time. It's that Alice won't welcome me there. She'll never say it directly, but a thousand little looks and gestures will make it obvious what she thinks of my outdated clothes, my old-fashioned manners, and every awkward word that comes from my mouth.

The haven I enjoy at my aunt's house, the one place where I'm never treated like an orphan and a burden, will become Alice Roosevelt's domain.

In the kitchen, I hand the tea tray over to Rosie, who assures me that she will slice chicken for our supper before she takes her evening off. Then, as the clock in the parlor chimes the quarter hour, I climb the front stairs to sit on the second-floor landing and wait for Uncle Valentine. It doesn't matter to him, but it makes me sad to think of him without anyone to mark his presence.

A minute later, the temperature drops, as if someone has opened a giant icebox. The ghost of my uncle, Valentine Hall III, appears at the bottom of the staircase and mounts the first step.

He looks frayed around the edges, like one of our tea towels. I can no longer read the label on the bottle of whiskey, and the shotgun over his shoulder is little more than a shadow. When he reaches the landing, I tilt my head to look up at him, wondering if he'll speak to me. Because Uncle Valentine died before I was born and his ghost is an Unaware, oblivious to his own death or anything since, he doesn't know who I am. Sometimes he says, "Hello, Annie," addressing me by my mother's name.

"Hello, Uncle Val," I whisper. "What are your thoughts on the education of girls?"

The ghost walks past me without acknowledging my

presence or my words. He's fading. Soon there will be nothing left of him but a ball of light making this trek upstairs, where Uncle Valentine planned, on his last day of life, to shoot pigeons from the attic window. After that, he'll disappear completely.

I drop my head back against the wall. In Alice's shadow, I feel the same way.

2

ALICE IN DISGRACE

*A*LICE Roosevelt sits in her aunt's front parlor on a recently reupholstered love seat. Her white shirtwaist is tailored; her mauve skirt, smartly pleated. Beside her rests her new hat—wide-brimmed, made of indigo felt to match the color of her winter coat, and trimmed with ostrich feathers because she likes to stand out in a crowd.

"Darling Alice," Aunt Bye says, sitting opposite on a lemon-colored chair. "I'm so happy to have you back. I think of this as your second home."

As far as Alice is concerned, this is her *first* home, and Aunt Bye, her first mother. But to Alice's dismay, the parlor, with its fresh wallpaper, new furniture, and electric lighting, is almost unrecognizable.

At least Aunt Bye, the woman who raised Alice for three years after her mother died, is the same as ever. Dark hair tucked into a bun, she lists slightly to the side, her body turned to favor the ear that wasn't deafened by childhood illness. She's quite a bit plumper than the last time Alice saw her, but other than that, pregnancy seems to suit her better than Alice's stepmother, who suffered greatly through all of hers.

"I suppose Mother Edith has told you terrible things about me," Alice says.

"Not *terrible*." Aunt Bye purses her lips. "But you can't deny you took advantage of her infirmity."

"I helped mind the children when she was confined to bed!"

"By encouraging them to sled down the staircase on dinner trays?"

"No one was seriously injured, and Teddy had a spare set of eyeglasses."

This statement is met by a snort. Alice's eyes wander over to the snorter—her new uncle, U.S. Navy Lieutenant Commander William Cowles, who, returning from carrying her suitcase upstairs, takes a stance behind his wife's chair. He winks, and Alice relaxes a bit, thinking she has an ally.

"Alice," Aunt Bye continues, "there will be rules and regulations here, and unlike the ones you ignored in Washington, I expect you to follow them. Do you understand?"

Alice snaps her attention back to her aunt and nods vigorously.

"You won't be tearing around as if every day is a great

party. Things need to be put back in their places. No hats left on the sofa to be sat upon."

Alice moves her ostrich-feathered hat to her lap.

"And I hope you will spend time with your cousin Eleanor. She has always had a calming influence on you."

Alice smiles blandly and doesn't commit one way or the other to time spent with "calming" Eleanor.

Folding her hands over her rounded stomach, Aunt Bye leans forward. "Now, I've said I won't allow you to treat every day like a party, but that doesn't mean we can't have some fun and even a great party now and then. Helen and Franklin have a winter break from school, so I've invited them to visit next week. My sister says she'll send Corinne as well."

"That's wonderful news!" Alice exclaims. Her twelve-year-old cousin, Corinne Robinson, visits Alice's family in Washington fairly often, but Alice hasn't seen her older, more distant cousins since the Roosevelt gathering at her father's home on Long Island last summer.

"Rules and regulations first." Aunt Bye raises her index finger. "I would hate to cancel these visits because of misbehavior."

"You won't have to," Alice promises.

Uncle Will clears his throat. "Let me escort you upstairs, Alice. I hope you like the way we've redecorated your room."

She would have preferred her room *not* be redecorated, but she follows Uncle Will upstairs without comment.

He reaches into Alice's old room and flips the switch that powers the new electric ceiling light. An incandescent filament flares and settles into a golden glow. The room looks smaller, lit from above. The wallpaper is new—rose and gray and patterned with peonies. She dislikes it instantly. But the furniture is the same, and her suitcase rests on top of her familiar bed.

"Do you like the change?" her uncle asks.

"Why, yes," she lies, setting her hat on the dresser.

"I'll leave you to unpack. The bathroom down the hall has new plumbing, although it takes a while to get the hot water going. Your aunt and I will be in the parlor if you care to join us later." Uncle Will withdraws from the room, pulling the door halfway closed.

Giving her privacy, but not shutting her in. Surprisingly thoughtful, this new uncle.

Alice sighs, sinking onto the bed next to her suitcase. *Home again.* And yet, not quite the home she craves. With Aunt Bye's new husband in the house and a baby on the way, Alice might once again end up as an extra appendage on a family that is sufficient without her.

A wriggling movement against her leg makes her jump. Oh! She almost forgot. Alice slips a hand into her skirt pocket and pulls out a twelve-inch length of slender green snake. "There you are," she coos. "How did you like your very first train ride?"

A red tongue flicks in and out.

"We'll have to be very good if we don't want to get sent

back to Mother Edith. You can help me with that, can't you?" Alice kisses the little snake and snaps open her suitcase with her free hand. Gently she lays Emily Spinach on top of her divided bicycling skirt.

Not in the mood to unpack just yet, Alice removes a single item from her suitcase and sets it on the bedside table—a framed photograph of her mother, Alice Hathaway Lee Roosevelt.

This photograph of her mother is the only one Alice has ever seen. Aunt Bye gave it to her, and in fact, everything she knows about her mother was told to her by her aunt. Her father never speaks of his first wife. He never even says her name, which means he avoids calling his daughter by the name they share. When he can't get out of calling her *something*, Father uses her family nickname, Sissy.

The Campaign of Terror (as Alice termed it in her head) had originally begun as a plan to gain her father's attention. Events escalated only because nothing she did mattered to him. The spitballs in the Capitol? Reported to Mother Edith. The cigar stubs she deliberately left for the laundress to find? Passed to Mother Edith.

It was when her stepmother threatened to send her to New York that Alice began to envision another end to this game. Encouraging her siblings to sled down the staircase hadn't done it. Nor had wrecking the bicycle. But blowing up that tree stump with firecrackers—a stroke of genius! Telegrams were flying between New York and Washington before the smoke had dissipated. Even then, Father gave her no more than a cursory goodbye, too engrossed in some letter he'd received from the secretary of the navy, to whom he had been appointed assistant. "The second-highest civilian position in the navy," Mother Edith often reminded Alice, as if that were far more important than being her father.

Alice looks around her room with a sigh. The new wallpaper is quite hideous, but she can live with it. She suspects she'll have more patience with a lot of things in a house where she is actually loved.

She has just decided to try out the bathroom's plumbing when a loud mechanical snap resonates in the hallway outside her room. The sound is followed by a blue glow visible beyond her half-open door.

Alice sticks her head into the hallway. The blue glow comes from an Edison Ghost Lamp on a table down the hall. Alice approaches it warily. Her family owns two such lamps, but she has never seen one activated before. Its bell-shaped bulb pulses with blue light powered by something stranger than gas, electricity, or oil.

The hair on the back of her neck stands on end. She looks right and left and sees nothing. Perhaps the lamp is malfunctioning? Then nausea rolls over her. A sensation akin to a shower of slugs crawls over her body, starting at the top of her head, dripping down her face, and oozing over her shoulders.

Alice wipes her cheek and finds nothing there. Her pulse surging, she backs toward the stairs, her eyes darting everywhere. Even with the blue glow illuminating the hallway, there are dark shadows in every corner.

Then she stiffens.

From within the darkest shadow, a place face watches Alice silently.

EDISON GHOST LAMP

Universally acknowledged as the best early-warning system for ghost eruptions, Edison's Ghost Lamp provides afford-able, practical protection for your family. This beacon of safety detects electromagnetic pulses that precede the eruption of a new haunting, allowing it to alert you in a timely fashion. GET OUT FAST AND GET OUT SAFELY.

3

ELEANOR ACTS ON IMPULSE

I'M washing the supper dishes in a bucket of water from the pump when Rosie bursts through the back kitchen door, returning from her evening out. Her lined face is drawn with worry. "Miss Eleanor! Did you hear? There's been a ghost eruption at your aunt's house. There are police-men outside the house and city diagnosticians inside. I saw them on my way home."

"An eruption?" Faded ghosts like my uncle are one thing, but newly erupted ones can be dangerous. "Is everyone all right? Maybe I should . . ." I swallow nervously. "I'd like to go and see."

"You *should* go. Your aunt and uncle were standing on the sidewalk with Miss Alice. Find out if they need anything."

I pull off the apron and hurry to the front of the house, where I fumble through the coatracks to find a coat and a bonnet.

Outside, it is bitter cold and dark, despite the streetlamps and the stars in their black tapestry above the city. It's after nine o'clock, and the people who are still out and about look at me curiously as I pass them by. They are probably wondering what a girl my age is doing out alone.

Grandmother will skin me alive if one of her neighbors recognizes me. There will be *letters*.

Grabbing my hair in handfuls, I twist it under my bonnet. I'm tall enough that I can pass for an adult, as long as I'm not wearing my hair down like a little girl. By the time I reach Aunt Bye's house, no one pays me any mind. There are indeed policemen on the street carrying lanterns and official-looking gentlemen in suits walking into and out of my aunt's house, which has electric lights shining through every window. If Grandmother were here, she would collapse from apoplexy at the extravagant illumination.

"Aunt Bye!" I locate my aunt on the sidewalk in front of the house. She wears a woolen shawl around her shoulders, held in place by Uncle Will's great arms.

"Eleanor, sweetheart, what are you doing here?"

Aunt Bye's embrace is as warm and welcoming as ever, never mind that we are standing in the street on a February evening. "What happened?" I ask.

"Our ghost lamp turned itself on. And Alice saw something in the upstairs hallway."

Letting go of Aunt Bye, I turn to my cousin, who stands nearby with a suitcase at her feet. "Hello, Alice."

"Eleanor," she replies. Alice is wearing an obviously new

coat and a matching hat with a ridiculous spray of ostrich feathers. They protrude almost a foot into the air above her head. I move forward to hug her, but she doesn't remove her hands from her fur muff. Feeling foolish, I stop short and pretend to be busy rubbing my own hands because I forgot to bring gloves. Alice is only a few months older than I am— and at least six inches shorter—but she always manages to make me feel like an awkward child with no social graces.

"Lieutenant Commander Cowles?" We all turn as a man approaches Uncle Will. "I'm Hampton Grier, senior diagnostician from the Manhattan Ghost Diagnostics Guild."

"Do you have results for us yet?" Uncle Will asks.

Mr. Grier wobbles his hand back and forth. "Some. There are definitely signs of an eruption. Temperature variations from room to room. Electromagnetic pulses. Ectoplasmic residue on the walls of the second-floor hallway. Visual and auditory irregularities. What we haven't seen, however, is any manifestation of the ghost itself. This is good news because Vengefuls tend to attack immediately."

"Does that mean we can go back inside?"

"Noooo." The diagnostician purses his lips. "Better to err on the side of caution. Even an Unaware can be hostile if they view *you* as an intruder in *their* home. Now, I was told that one of the household members saw a manifestation at the time of the eruption?"

"I saw a face," Alice volunteers. "In a corner of the hallway. Just for a second, after the ghost lamp went on."

Mr. Grier glances briefly at Alice, then addresses Uncle

Will. "Did it speak to her? Were there any sounds at all? Did it move or cause objects to move?"

Uncle Will waves a hand at Alice. "Ask my niece. She can answer for herself."

With a frown, Mr. Grier looks down on Alice as if Uncle Will has just invited him to interview one of the lamp poles. "Think carefully, little girl," he says. "Did the ghost say or do anything? Make objects move? Throw things at your head? Try to remember."

Alice scowls. "I remember *exactly* what happened, and I would have told you in the first place if it threw anything at my head! It made no noise, and it was gone so quickly, I can't tell you if it was a man or a woman. *But*," she adds, "it appeared at my eye level, so maybe it was the ghost of some-one my age."

Mr. Grier mumbles that he'll take her opinion under consideration and turns back to Uncle Will. "I cannot clear your house for habitation until we've diagnosed the ghost. Neither you nor your servants can reenter, but if you wish, my associates will retrieve whatever belongings you need for the night."

Uncle Will and Aunt Bye consult each other silently.

"You can stay at Grandmother Hall's." The words pop out of my mouth before I've thought them through, and immediately, my cheeks burn with embarrassment. Grand-mother will be livid if I bring them all home with me. Think of the gas lamps they'll light!

Aunt Bye smiles as if she can read the dismay on my face.

"Thank you, Eleanor. But Maisie and Ida have family they can stay with, and Will and I will go to a hotel. Of course, Alice would probably like to spend the night with you. Isn't that right, Alice?"

Alice looks at me, her forehead rumpled, and then she looks at the two servant girls, Maisie and Ida, as if wondering whether it would be possible to go with them instead. When she faces me again, however, she smiles in such a friendly way, I might have imagined her initial hesitation.

But I know I didn't.

❧ 4 ❧

ALICE IN THE HALL HOUSE

ALICE would rather spend the night almost any-where than with Eleanor. But the wriggling of Emily Spinach in her pocket reminds her of her promise to be good. She accepts the offer, and she and Eleanor walk the three blocks to Mrs. Hall's gloomy house. *It could be worse. With any luck, the old bat will already be asleep in bed.*

But the evening continues its downward spiral when they find Mrs. Hall waiting inside the foyer of her home, blocking the hallway like a siege engine. She starts talking as soon as Eleanor crosses the threshold.

"I could not believe my ears when Rosie told me you went out! What in the world possessed you to go to your aunt's home at this time of—" Seeing Alice behind Eleanor, Mrs. Hall stops cold. Her eyes narrow, and her lips press together while she no doubt pins the blame for Eleanor's behavior on Alice. Then her gaze drops to Alice's suitcase, and her lips disappear altogether, sucked right into her face.

Hurriedly, Eleanor explains Alice's presence, untying her hideous bonnet. Down tumbles her hair, and Alice can't help but admire it.

Eleanor's life is hard, worse than Alice's. Her mother and one of her brothers died of diphtheria when she was eight years old, and shortly after that, her father died too, leaving Eleanor and little Gracie to be raised by their horrible grandmother (who is no relation to Alice, thank heavens!). It's no wonder Eleanor is timid and awkward and blends into the wallpaper if she stands still too long. There's only one thing about Eleanor that is truly notable—and that's her hair. Glossy and thick and the color of golden wheat, it hangs past her waist. Alice would steal it if she could.

By the time Eleanor has hung up her bonnet and coat and taken Alice's as well, she has explained to her grandmother that Alice will be staying only until morning.

"You don't know that," Mrs. Hall says ominously, which makes Alice squirm. What if the diagnosticians need more than one night to categorize the haunting? Alice might be stuck here! Then Mrs. Hall poses an even worse possibility. "Your aunt may have to move. Many people do, after a ghost eruption."

The idea jolts Alice. In the rush to grab her suitcase and her snake and vacate the house, that thought hadn't occurred to her. "Surely not!" she exclaims. "There's only a one-in-three chance it's a Vengeful!"

"What a *terrible* thing." Eleanor's grandmother clucks her tongue. "And the house just redecorated too. So much money wasted. Alice, you must be exhausted after your travels. Eleanor, take your cousin up to your room and put her to bed."

The house hasn't changed since the last time Alice was here. Dark, with gaslights turned as low as they will go, and furniture that . . . well, *looms* is the only word that truly describes it. *This* is the house that should be haunted, and of course it *is*, but only by the ghost of Eleanor's uncle, who got soused and fell out an attic window twenty years ago.

There isn't any indoor plumbing, and the only privy is in the basement. At night, residents use a chamber pot, which they are expected to empty themselves down the basement privy in the morning. Alice sorely wishes she'd had the chance to use Aunt Bye's new upstairs toilet!

In Eleanor's room, the girls change into their bedclothes. Alice's nightgown is soft cotton with ruffles and bows. Eleanor's is plain gray flannel.

"You don't think Aunt Bye will have to move, do you?" Eleanor asks.

How should I know? Alice almost snaps, but catches herself just in time. "I don't think so," she says in a reasonable tone. "That man said a Vengeful would have attacked at once."

"You mean that man who called you a little girl?" Eleanor says. "I thought you were going to kick him in the shins."

Alice gives her cousin an appraising glance, surprised that

such a thought would occur to perfect, "calming" Eleanor. "It crossed my mind."

A Vengeful ghost would be a disaster. Aunt Bye would have to find a new house, and Alice would likely be shipped back to Washington, D.C., on the earliest possible train. Since she knows perfectly well that she has burned her bridges with Mother Edith and that Father doesn't care one way or the other, Alice's next stop would probably be a boarding school.

But the ghost didn't attack her. It stared at her from the shadows for a single second before vanishing, leaving Alice alone and unharmed in the eerie blue glow of the Edison Lamp. Doesn't that mean it *can't* be a Vengeful?

The knot that formed in her chest when Mrs. Hall made her prediction unravels a bit, and the idea of being stuck here overnight with Eleanor, using chamber pots and a privy, seems more tolerable. With that settled in her mind, Alice looks around the bedroom, her skirt folded over one arm, and considers what to do with Emily Spinach.

Sitting on the edge of the bed, Eleanor begins braiding her wheaten hair. "Even if it's not a Vengeful, a newly erupted ghost is frightening."

"I thought you were used to sharing a house with a ghost."

"It's not the same. Uncle Val is nearly faded away." Eleanor's eyes gaze across the room, softly focused, while her fingers weave a long plait as thick as Alice's arm. "Sometimes

I wish Elliott would erupt as a ghost. I know it wouldn't really be my brother, but I miss him. And Father. Of course, Father didn't die in this house, so he wouldn't erupt here even if . . ." She breaks off and glances at Alice. "Is that a terrible thing to wish for?"

"No. I don't think it is." Alice doesn't blame Eleanor for wanting to see her brother and father again, even as ghosts. But she notices that Eleanor doesn't wish for her mother to return.

Two things about Eleanor's mother stand out in Alice's memory. The first is that she was very, very beautiful. The second is that she constantly criticized Eleanor, telling her to keep her lips closed to hide her crooked teeth. Once, when Eleanor stamped her foot and showed a little temper—a rare thing for her—her mother chastised her, saying, "You have no looks, so see to it that you have manners."

Alice's family situation is not ideal, but she has to admit that the one thing worse than a mother who died before you knew her is a mother who disliked you when she was alive.

Eleanor turns off the gas lamp, and the girls pull up the blanket and settle into bed. Alice must have been more tired than she thought because she doesn't have another coherent thought until a loud screech jars her awake.

Pale morning sunlight streams through the windows, and Eleanor is staring into one of her dresser drawers, both hands pressed against her mouth.

"Oh." Alice rubs her eyes and hides her smirk. "Eleanor, meet Emily Spinach. Emily Spinach, meet Eleanor."

TYPES OF GHOSTS AND HOW THEY FADE:

A CHILD'S PRIMER

BY J. M. MASON & A. STEELE

Ghosts erupt, and no one knows why. Most persons die and never return as a ghost. Some persons return a few years after their death. Others appear after decades or centuries have passed.

There are three types of ghosts: Friendlies, Unawares, and Vengefuls. There is no way to predict what type of ghost a person will leave behind.

Friendlies are ghosts who interact with the living in harmless ways.

Unawares do not understand that they are dead. They might or might not interact with the living.

Vengefuls are ghosts who intentionally seek to harm the living.

Over time, ghosts fade and disappear. The time needed for a ghost to fade varies, but fading can be encouraged by the removal of anything in the house to which the ghost has a personal attachment. If the ghost is a family member and the haunting is troublesome, it may be advisable for the family to move and sell the house to strangers. In extreme cases, only the destruction of the house will cause the ghost to fade.

Please note: The authors of this text have simplified information for the sake of children's education. The authors are not responsible for death, injury, or mental anguish caused by a haunting or by readers following these guidelines.

5

ELEANOR EAVESDROPS

ALICE doesn't seem to think there's anything wrong with stashing her snake in my unmentionables. I don't want her to think I'm afraid of it, so even though I'll have to wash everything in that drawer after she leaves, I pretend I don't mind. After breakfast, I find an old hatbox to make a better home, and we fill it with fabric scraps. Rosie gives us a bit of raw fish without asking why—although she does look at us strangely.

After the snake is settled and, thankfully, out of my sight, Alice offers to brush my hair, which surprises me. I hand her the hairbrush, and she unwinds my braid and runs the bristles from the top of my scalp to the ends of my hair. At first, I feel awkward, as if I should try to make conversation, but I don't know what to say to Alice. I never have. As the silence goes on, I start to relax, remembering how my father used to brush my hair like this.

"You know who likes your hair?" Alice's voice breaks into my memories.

I think *Alice* likes my hair. "Who?"

"Cousin Franklin."

I whirl around so quickly, she drops the brush. "Please don't tease me, Alice."

She blinks in surprise, and then her expression sours. "I *wasn't*, Eleanor."

Someone raps on my door. "Miss Eleanor?" Rosie calls. "Your auntie Bye sent a note. Their ghost is a Friendly, and Miss Alice can go home."

Alice and I exchange glances. Quickly, I pin up my hair while she gathers her things. I'm going with her. I want to see this Friendly ghost, if it will show itself! Alice gives me Emily Spinach's box to carry and puts the snake in a pocket to keep it warm. "You have pockets in your skirt?" I have never seen such a thing.

"I pestered Mother Edith until she told our seamstress to put pockets in all my skirts. Boys get to carry their belongings with them. Why not girls?"

That is a good question. Now I feel not only unfashionable in the clothing that once belonged to my mother's sisters, but also downtrodden.

Alice leads the way, bumping her suitcase down the steps. I follow with the hatbox until our progress is blocked by Grandmother. "Well, Alice, I hope you enjoyed your stay as my guest."

I cringe at this obvious invitation for Alice to thank her

for her hospitality, which consisted of a bed to share and a sparsely buttered slice of toast.

Alice puts on a smile that is both hard to find fault with and utterly false. "Thank you, Mrs. Hall. It was very kind of you to take me in last night."

"Yes, it was," Grandmother agrees. "Where are *you* going, Eleanor? Surely Alice knows the way. There's no reason for you to accompany her."

"I . . ." *I want to see the new ghost.* "I have to carry the snake's box."

Grandmother tilts her head, presenting one ear in a way that suggests she must have misheard me. *"Whose box?"*

"The snake's box." Alice draws the creature out of her pocket and holds it up for Grandmother to see in all its brilliant green, twelve-inch, dangling glory.

Grandmother staggers backward, like an umbrella caught in a gust of wind. Alice flashes me a grin and charges past her toward the front door.

"Eleanor!" Grandmother roars, rounding on me. *"You allowed that girl to bring a reptile into my home?"*

"I'm taking it away now!" I hurry after my cousin. "Back later!"

As soon as the door is shut behind us, I look awkwardly at Alice. "Thank you."

"For what?"

I don't understand her. A few minutes ago, she was teasing me about our cousin Franklin, and now she's rescued me from Grandmother for no reason that I can fathom.

The police and the city diagnosticians are gone when we reach Aunt Bye's house. Except for the excess trash in the gutters (waxed-paper sandwich wrappers and cigar butts), it's as if nothing happened here. As soon as we set foot inside, however, that illusion vanishes. Before our eyes, the front hall telescopes out to an impossible length, stretching like taffy until it appears longer than a city block. "Jumpin' Jehosaphat," Alice gasps. Her voice echoes, but in a different timbre, as if someone at the other end of the hall is calling her words back to her.

I take a cautious step forward on the black-and-white parquet floor. My eyes tell me that the tiles are squirming and shifting despite the floor feeling solid beneath my feet. I try to walk in a straight line, but my hip bumps one of Aunt Bye's hall tables hard enough to bruise. Biting back an exclamation, I plunk down Emily Spinach's box. Alice can claim it later. I need both hands to navigate.

"Hello?" Aunt Bye's voice floats out of the parlor. "Who's there?"

"It's me!" Alice calls. "And Eleanor."

Uncle Will appears in the doorway to the parlor. At first he seems terribly far away, but when he holds out one hand to me and the other to Alice, he reaches us instantly and pulls us both into the parlor. Two seconds later, Alice and I are sitting on the sofa, trying to regain our equilibrium. I pull off my bonnet and fan my face with it.

"Horrible, isn't it?" says Aunt Bye.

"Is it like this all over the house?" I ask. "Is it going to stay this way?"

Uncle Will runs a hand over his bald head. "Only in the front hall and a little bit of the second floor. That diagnostician, Mr. Grier, said these eruption effects are normal and will recede in the first day. Then we'll only have a 'regular' haunted house." He gives us a crooked smile and adds doubtfully, "Hooray?"

"What made them decide it was a Friendly ghost?" Alice unpins her hat.

"The diagnosticians stayed all night, waiting for the ghost to reveal itself," Uncle Will explains. "At dawn they heard a whistling noise from the kitchen, which turned out to be the teakettle. The ghost made them tea."

"How do they know it wasn't an Unaware, making tea for itself?"

"There were five investigators, and they found five teacups set out on the table, with five teaspoons and a sugar bowl."

My skin prickles. The image is both disturbing and charming. I wonder if that's usual for a Friendly ghost: attempting to behave like a human. "Have you seen it?"

Aunt Bye shakes her head. "We haven't seen or heard a thing except for the wobbly front hallway. It hasn't made me a cup of tea either, more's the pity."

Uncle Will chuckles. "*I'll* fetch you tea. I'm not sure I trust refreshments offered by a supernatural phantasm."

Alice jumps to her feet. "Can we go upstairs? I want to look at the place where I saw the ghost."

"I suppose you can." Aunt Bye turns up her palm. "The diagnosticians declared the house Safe for Habitation."

"C'mon!" Alice drags me to my feet.

"Be careful, girls!" Aunt Bye calls after us.

The hallway looks normal again, but I don't trust it and walk gingerly. Alice pulls on my arm, hurrying as always, although in this instance being taller helps. I slow her down.

Climbing the staircase isn't a problem until I realize there are more stairs than there should be. Alice stumbles at the top, trying to put her foot down on a step that doesn't exist. Learning from her example, I close my eyes, grip the banister, and feel with my feet until I find the landing. Only when I'm firmly established on the second floor do I open my eyes.

"Smart of you," Alice says, rubbing her knee. Then she points. "That's the ghost lamp."

My eyes follow her finger. It isn't lighted now. Edison Lamps detect eruptions, not the ghost that remains afterward.

Alice's finger shifts. "I was in my room. I came out, saw the light, and started walking toward it. Then I saw his face over there." She points at the farthest corner of the hallway.

"His? Last night you said you couldn't tell if it was male or female."

Alice turns to me, her eyes wide. "I couldn't! So why do I say his now? I'm not sure. Was it a silly slip? Or something else?"

I stare at her. If she doesn't know, who does?

Alice stalks down the hall, focused on that corner near

the enclosed back stairs the servants use. "Eleanor, come see this!" She points out a white, sticky residue on the wall.

"Is that . . ."

"Ectoplasm." Alice sticks out a finger.

"Don't touch it!"

She puts her index finger into the center of it, then looks at the tip of her finger, sniffs it, and holds it out to me. "Smell that."

"No, thank you!"

Alice wipes her finger on her expensive-looking skirt. "Well, thank you for carrying Emily's box. I suppose I should say goodbye and unpack now."

I take a step backward, feeling pushed away.

Is it because I wouldn't smell the ectoplasm? Or had she tired of me before that?

This is exactly what I expected from Alice. I should have known that spending one night at my house wouldn't change anything between us. To Alice, I have always been one of those tedious tasks that, as a matter of courtesy, you can't put aside—like writing a thank-you note—although you wish you could and, as a result, spend as little time with it as possible.

"Goodbye, then, Alice." Whirling away from her, I hurry downstairs, my cheeks aflame. I almost go straight out the front door, but it would hurt Aunt Bye's feelings if I left without saying goodbye. The hallway doesn't play tricks on me this time, and I pause outside the parlor door to give my blush time to fade.

On the other side of the door, Uncle Will is speaking. "I think we should sell the house."

"We'll never get back the money we put into renovations," Aunt Bye objects. "Not with a new haunting, even if it is a Friendly."

"The money is not important. You and the baby are."

"I don't *want* to sell this house. I've had it since Alice was born."

Uncle Will sighs. "To be honest, having Alice here is part of what worries me."

I put my hand over my mouth, surprised to hear this from my good-natured uncle.

"Will! I could never turn her away!"

"No, of course not. But I wish she had come *after* the baby was born. I'm afraid her presence here is going to remind you of what happened all those years ago. And now this ghost . . ." Uncle Will breaks off and then continues. "There are too many parallels for my peace of mind. Will you consider *renting* another house until after the baby is born? We can close this one up and hope the ghost fades quickly."

There's a long pause while Aunt Bye thinks it over. "I suppose that's a possibility."

"Good. I'll write our solicitor and have him inquire about a suitable place."

After that, there is silence, and deciding that the conversation is over, I open the door. At the precise moment I walk in, Aunt Bye says to her husband, "Poor, poor Alice. You have no idea what it was like."

Uncle Will takes her hand. "I can't even imagine."

Then they both look up and see me. "Eleanor!" my aunt gasps.

I'm not sure if *poor, poor Alice* refers to the baby who lost her mother or to the mother who died. But what puzzles me more is why my aunt and uncle look so stricken. Aunt Bye pales at the sight of me, as if terrified that I overheard what she said.

But why?

I know what happened when Alice was born. Her mother died shortly afterward from kidney disease, and a few days later our grandmother, Martha Roosevelt, died of an unrelated case of typhoid fever.

At least, that's what I was *told* happened.

6

ALICE MEETS A
CELEBRATED WOMAN

WHEN the doorbell rings in the midafternoon, Alice rushes past Maisie to answer it. The ghost has not made an appearance all day, and Alice wishes something interesting would happen. To her gratification, the woman on the other side of the door looks as though she might serve the purpose.

She's not a young woman—in her thirties, probably—attractive, with bright brown eyes and dark hair tucked under an extremely fashionable hat. "Good afternoon. Are your parents at home?"

"My aunt and uncle are in. They're the ones who live here." Stepping back, Alice invites the woman to enter. "Who shall I say is calling?"

The woman strips off a glove and offers Alice her hand to shake. "Mrs. Elizabeth Cochrane Seaman. I represent the New York City Supernatural Registry."

Maisie hovers nearby, consternated by Alice's usurping her duties, and then disappears to announce the visitor, leaving Alice to wait with Mrs. Seaman in the foyer. Alice tries (and fails) not to stare. The woman's face is familiar, although Alice is fairly certain they have never met. "May I take your coat and hat?"

The visitor unpins her hat, hands it to Alice, and is just removing her coat when the floor undulates beneath them. Alice grabs the coatrack for balance, but Mrs. Seaman plants her feet and stands firm. "Well!" she exclaims when the phenomenon ends. "You certainly do have a powerful eruption here! Don't worry. These effects won't last long."

Maisie reappears. "This way, Mrs. Seaman."

Alice hangs up the hat and coat and scurries after them, arriving in the parlor just after Mrs. Seaman finishes introducing herself again.

Uncle Will shakes her hand. "I'm Lieutenant Commander William Cowles, and this is my wife, Anna Roosevelt Cowles."

"But everyone calls me Bye." The visitor raises one arched eyebrow, and Aunt Bye explains. "When I was younger, my sister and brothers claimed that I was so busy, coming and going, that the only thing they were able to say to me was *Bye, Anna! Bye!*"

Everyone chuckles at the story and chooses a place to sit. Uncle Will opens the conversation by saying what Alice is thinking. "You look very familiar, Mrs. Seaman. Have we met?"

"I don't think so, Commander Cowles. But it is probable that you know me under my pen name. I used to write for the *New York World*."

"Nellie Bly!" Alice and her uncle cry out at the same time.

Nellie Bly, the famed investigative reporter, smiles demurely and snaps open her reticule to remove a small leather-bound journal.

Of course! Alice should have known—*would* have known, if she hadn't been thrown by the name Elizabeth Cochrane Seaman. Sitting in this parlor is the most famous female journalist in the world! And she is here to . . . what? "You gave up being a reporter to work for the Supernatural Registry?" Alice blurts out. "You collect data for the city now? Instead of setting world records and uncovering corruption in our industries?"

"Alice!" Aunt Bye exclaims.

Miss Bly doesn't seem to mind the impertinence. "I'm a volunteer with the board. I retired from the *New York World* because my husband is an invalid and I need to stay close to home. Public service keeps me busy." She winks at Alice. "I might also be working on a groundbreaking book about ghost eruptions."

Alice brightens. Now *that* sounds more like Nellie Bly!

Miss Bly asks for basic facts about the eruption: date, time, location, physical manifestations, and supernatural phenomena. "I saw the front hallway," she says wryly.

Alice repeats her experience at the time of the eruption,

and Uncle Will explains the incident that caused the diagnosticians to label the ghost a Friendly. Miss Bly nods, making notes in shorthand. "Has the ghost done anything else?"

Aunt Bye starts to say no—but cuts off the word prematurely as the temperature in the room plummets. Her breath fogs in the air. Alice sits up attentively.

The drapes in the front window shuffle apart, slowly, jerkily, casting a patch of sunlight onto Nellie Bly's journal. Cocking her head, Miss Bly gazes at the drapes. "Why, hello there. It's nice of you to join us."

Instantly, the room's temperature returns to normal. Alice glances at her aunt and uncle. They look at each other and then at her. Uncle Will gives an exaggerated shudder. Aunt Bye laughs nervously.

Miss Bly turns back to her notes as if she encounters these manifestations every day. "Do you know who the progenitor of the ghost is?"

Aunt Bye shakes her head. "We don't. Alice thinks it might be a child, based on the glimpse she had. But we aren't certain."

"Do you know the history of the house? Any child deaths?"

"I know the people I bought the house from. All their children lived to adulthood."

"A servant's child, perhaps? You said the eruption occurred near the servants' staircase."

"That I wouldn't know."

Miss Bly inserts her pencil into the journal and closes

it. "If you *can* identify the progenitor, you might be able to encourage the ghost to fade. Learn what anchors the ghost to this house—be it an object, a room, even a scent—and eradicate it."

Alice flinches at the word *eradicate*. It sounds so vicious.

"The house has recently been modernized," Uncle Will says. "We extended the plumbing to the second floor and installed electric wiring throughout. That involved tearing into the walls and repapering every room. Then we bought new draperies"—he glances fondly at Bye—"and some new furniture. To go with the new color scheme, I was told. Even the furniture that we didn't change—well, I wasn't around when Bye bought the house, but I can't imagine she kept the furniture of past residents."

"No." Aunt Bye holds up a finger. "But it occurs to me that there are many items in the attic left by previous occupants."

"I'd start there if I were you." Miss Bly opens her reticule again, inserts the journal, and removes a calling card. "If you discover anything more about your ghost, please contact me at my office. I will update our records so that we have an accurate registry of this haunting."

"Thank you," Uncle Will says. "Perhaps I should mention that we will soon be vacating the premises. For a few months, at least. Until my wife delivers our child."

Alice blinks. *What?*

"Understandable," Miss Bly replies. "New ghosts can be disturbing in their intensity, even if they are Friendly.

Friendly is a bit of a misnomer anyway, as a category name. All it means is that the ghost is aware enough to interact with the living, but not in a dangerous way. They aren't always *friendly*. Some are mischievous, some are shy, and some can be downright cantankerous. You and your wife should do what makes you comfortable."

And will I go with them, or back to Washington? Alice's eyes dart around the room. She didn't like Miss Bly's use of the word *eradicate*, but if it comes to her needs versus the ghost's existence . . .

She jumps to her feet. "I will investigate this haunting!" Aunt Bye and Uncle Will exchange a glance, like amused parents, which irks Alice. So she addresses Nellie Bly. "I can research past occupants of the house and look through the attic for the ghost's belongings." Well, she'll search the attic, anyway. She has someone else in mind for the tedious research part.

"There is no guarantee it will fade the haunting any faster, but in my experience, it never hurts to try." Miss Bly rises from her chair.

"You can count on me." Alice shoots a look at her aunt and uncle, telegraphing her sincerity.

No ghost is going to dislodge her from her home. It will have to be the other way around.

Dear Eleanor,

I shall be investigating the haunting of Aunt Bye's house with the ghoal (I did not misspell that, it is on purpose) of identifying the progenitor of the ghost, locating any of his (or her) belongings, and disposing of them. If we cannot encourage this ghost to fade quickly, Uncle Will is going to close up the house and move. I do not know where the new place will be, but it seems doubtful that it will be within walking distance of your grandmother's house. You probably do not want them to move any more than I do, which is why I know you will help.

    I will inventory the contents of the attic, and you can search library records for clues about the previous inhabitants.

Your cousin Alice

P.S. Aunt Bye purchased the house in 1884 from a Mr. and Mrs. Andrew Morrow. We called upon Mrs. Morrow at their new residence last evening, and she says there were no deaths in the house in the thirty years she lived there. She does not remember the name of the person who sold the house to her husband, and sadly her husband does not remember his own name most days, let alone anyone else's.

P.P.S. The date on the cornerstone of the house is 1825, in case you have not noticed.

~ 7 ~

ALICE IN THE ATTIC

AFTER dispatching Ida to hand-deliver her letter to Eleanor, Alice sets about her own task. Because the electric lighting in the house does not extend into the attic, she takes an oil lantern to light her way.

The circular servants' staircase continues past the second-floor landing and ends at an overhead door. Alice unjams the latch and shoves the heavy door upward. When it reaches the tipping point, it falls away from her and strikes the attic floor with a *whomp,* raising a cloud of dust. Chilled air seeps into the stairwell. Mounting the three final steps, she climbs into the upper story.

The peaked ceiling slants sharply downward on both sides. Two small, grimy windows provide next to no illumination, but by the light of her lantern, Alice can see that the attic is full to bursting with decades' worth of discarded items.

A linen press. A dressmaker's dummy. A tarnished mirror. There are stacked cardboard boxes, frames without pictures, and a tall curio cabinet. She spies a rocking chair with a broken runner, several bolts of moth-eaten fabric, and a stack of old magazines tied with string. There are trunks and a mismatched cluster of luggage. Alice will have to go through them all.

She heaves a sigh. Maybe she gave the better task to Eleanor.

Where in the world should I start?

With Pepsin chewing gum, of course. Removing a package from her pocket, she unwraps two sticks—and then one more because this looks like a three-stick job.

The trunks, she discovers, are full of clothes: men's suits riddled with holes, yellowed petticoats, heaps of dry-rotted stockings, and old shoes. None of them appear to be the right size for a child.

A metal box decorated with faded paint turns out to be a toy chest, which is more promising. Alice exhales in satisfaction—and her breath turns to fog in the chilly air. Uneasily, she glances around. The lantern casts shadows on the walls and the slanted ceiling, but she sees no movement and hears no sound except her own breathing. Nevertheless, Alice feels in the primitive depths of her brain that something is watching her. "Hello?" she whispers.

Nothing.

Her chewing gum has gone dry too soon. She spits out the wad, sticks it on the back of the tarnished mirror, and returns her attention to the toy chest. Inside she finds a drum, a fife, and a doll with a china face and movable eyelids. When Alice picks up the doll, it blinks at her. Tin soldiers, dominoes, and playing cards lie loose in the bottom of the box. Alice rummages through them until a creaking sound causes her to whip around.

The broken rocker is rocking. It shouldn't be able to rock on that splintered runner, but it is. Her lantern throws a skewed shadow of the impossibly rocking chair across the floor and onto the sloping ceiling above.

Alice's body trembles with a shiver not entirely caused by the cold. "Are these your toys?"

No answer. The rocker stops.

Blowing on her hands to warm them, Alice moves on to one of the cardboard boxes and lifts the lid. Inside are a number of smaller boxes, and curled on top of them is a huge black snake.

Alice sets the box lid aside and considers the creature. She's not terribly surprised to find a snake in the attic, but how did it get inside a closed box? How does it eat? It doesn't look dead—although it does lie absolutely still. Then she understands.

She looks at the rocking chair again. It's motionless, as though waiting for her reaction. "If you're trying to disturb me, you'll have to do better than that. I'm not the kind of girl who screams at the sight of a snake."

When she turns back to the box, the snake is gone.

Some are mischievous, Nellie Bly said of so-called Friendly ghosts. *Some can be downright cantankerous.* Alice feels a grow-ing certainty that their unwanted visitor is a boy.

The smaller boxes inside the large one are filled with let-ters addressed to the Morrows, the people Aunt Bye bought the house from. Nothing to do with the ghost's progenitor, then.

Alice pushes the box aside and stamps her feet. Her legs have gone stiff with cold, and her teeth are beginning to chatter. She hasn't been in the attic long enough for the temperature to drop as much as it has. That *thing* is to blame, turning her into an icicle with its unnatural coldness.

Does it know what I'm doing? Is that why it's watching me?

It made tea for the investigators. Opened the drapes for Nellie Bly. But Alice got a snake.

It knows I want to make it fade. To eradicate it.

Too bad, Alice decides. *It already had its life. I'm not going to let it wreck mine.*

A second cardboard box is filled to the brim with papers that look like legal documents. The one on top appears to be some kind of loan from a bank. The next two say something about insurance. Hurriedly, she riffles through the papers without removing or reading them, looking for something more interesting.

A whoosh of displaced air warns Alice barely a sec-ond before a pile of boxes behind her topples over, spilling the contents everywhere. Alice stares at the mess. Did she bump those boxes herself? Or did something else give them a push? Old photographs are pooled around her feet, and for a moment, she thinks that maybe the ghost is *giving* her what she needs to identify him.

But she recognizes the young man in the first photograph she picks up. It's her father, looking young and handsome and much thinner than he is today. The next one is her deceased uncle Elliott—Eleanor's father—posing with his two sisters, her aunts Bye and Corinne. Alice shuffles through the other photographs, finding various groupings of her relations: her father and Uncle Elliott together in bathing costumes, and an especially nice portrait of her grandparents, Theodore and Martha Roosevelt. Sadly, Alice never met either of them.

Or, more accurately, she never met her grandfather. It is possible that Grandmother Martha had an opportunity to see Alice, at least from the doorway of her room. She died of typhoid fever only a couple of days after Alice was born and never held her infant granddaughter for fear of infecting her.

Your mother held you, though, Aunt Bye assured Alice when she told her this story. *She only had a day with you before she passed, but you were never out of her arms.*

Alice looks through the photographs one more time but does not find any of her mother. She slips the entire stack into the pocket of her divided skirt. They shouldn't be in this damp and dusty attic. Aunt Bye must have forgotten about them. Crouching on the floor, Alice starts putting the other spilled items back into the fallen boxes. Mostly they are old books and primers and what looks like a school report for Aunt Corinne. There are a few letters in envelopes, and one sheet of paper by itself that almost gets buried beneath a stack of other things—except that Alice spots her name on the page and stops to look at it.

It's part of a letter, the last page of a letter to be precise, because it starts in the middle of a sentence and ends with Uncle Elliott's signature.

is hard to understand, I know. It isn't that he doesn't love her, because he does. You know that. But grief and love and anger— yes, _anger_ at the unfairness of it all—make for a strange combination. If Teddy has to exile himself to the Dakotas, rustling cows until he comes to terms with their deaths, then so be it.

And yes, dear Bye, I know rustlers are thieves and Teddy is herding steers, not cows, but I hope that my blatant disregard for the proper usage of terms has provoked at least a glimmer of a smile from you in this time of sorrow.

Teddy will come home when he is ready. In the meantime, concentrate on giving all your love to that precious baby, and allow our brother the freedom to grieve and tend his own heart. No matter how much he loves Alice, he also blames her for the tragedy, and therein lies the problem.

Fondly,
Elliott

Alice reads it twice, her fingers numb with cold and her body shivering. This letter is about *her*. *She* is the precious baby in Aunt Bye's care. The *tragedy*, the *time of sorrow*—that refers to the deaths of her mother and her grandmother. She never knew that her father ran off to the Dakotas and simply *abandoned* his newborn daughter with his sister.

He was angry. Grieving, which is understandable. But also *angry*.

No matter how much he loves Alice, he also blames her for the tragedy, and therein lies the problem.

Tears blur her vision, and, over the pounding of her pulse, a persistent creaking assaults her ears. She turns around, clutching Uncle Elliott's letter against her chest.

The creaking chair rocks faster now, still empty. But the shadow on the sloping ceiling has changed. In the shadow, the chair distinctly contains an occupant—the silhouette of a boy with knee-length pants, drooping socks, and shoes.

Alice's muscles lock as if frozen in a block of ice.

The shadow boy's face is in profile, but as Alice watches, that changes. The silhouette is absorbed into the featureless head as some unseen thing in the chair turns its face toward Alice. *You came into this world, and two souls left it. The two women your father loved best. He must have wished you had never been born.*

Where do those words come from? They appear in her mind as if whispered to her. But she doesn't hear them. She thinks them. Alice is telling herself what she has always known inside, and what her aunt and uncle knew too. She came into this attic searching for the ghost's history, and instead she has found her own.

If you're trying to disturb me, you'll have to do better than that, she challenged the ghost only a few minutes ago. *I'm not the kind of girl who screams at the sight of a snake.*

It seems her challenge was accepted.

Suddenly, the rocker stops moving. The shadow vanishes, and the temperature begins to rise, returning to the normal chill of an unheated attic in February. But Alice can't stop shaking. Snatching up her lantern, she kicks boxes aside in her rush to get to the hole in the floor and down through it, pulling the heavy door closed behind her. There will be no more searching the attic today.

Score one for the ghost; zero for Alice.

8

ELEANOR'S DISCOVERY

*M*Y first impulse after reading Alice's letter is to rip it up and burn it on the kitchen stove.

Why does Alice think she can submit orders to me as if I were her maid? As if she were a *captain* in the army, and I a lowly private. Yesterday, she dismissed me from her presence when she was tired of me, and now she's summoning me back because she needs me to do something she doesn't know how to do—or doesn't want to do—herself.

But, from what I overheard yesterday, Uncle Will *does* want to move out of that house, and Alice is correct about how that will affect me. Grandmother Hall has done all she can to separate me from my Roosevelt relatives, but even she can't deny me visits with an aunt who lives three blocks away. If Aunt Bye and Uncle Will move, my visits with them might cease.

I also feel a little thrill over Alice's use of the word *clues.*

This is a mystery, and I have never solved a mystery more complicated than where Grandmother left her reading spectacles. I am certain that Alice assigned me the library research because it's the slow, plodding kind of work that she hates . . . but I love the library. It *is* better suited to me.

Grandmother gives me permission without my having to beg or wheedle. The library is one of the few places she lets me go on my own. The head librarian, Mrs. Adams, greets me cheerily, and when I explain the purpose for my visit, she sets me up at a table in the reference section with pencils, paper, and a quick lesson on using the census registry.

If Aunt Bye bought the house in 1884 and the Morrows lived there for thirty years before that, the previous owners would have sold the place in approximately 1854. The census is only taken every ten years, however, so I start with the ledger for 1850. A woman named Ella Drummond resided with her son at my aunt's address, 132 East Twenty-First Street, in that year, and when I check the 1840 and 1830 ledgers, I see that the Drummond family occupied the house for decades and that many children lived there over that time. The census record doesn't establish whether any of them died in childhood, but this is a promising start.

I copy down the names of the Drummonds, their ages at the time of each census, and their relationships to one another. Finding out when they died will be the next step. I'll ask Mrs. Adams where that information can be found, but I suspect she'll point me to the local churches for their parish burial records.

Even though I have what I came for, I dawdle putting the ledgers back on their shelves, thinking about the conversation I overheard between Aunt Bye and Uncle Will. At first I thought I understood what my uncle meant when he said that having Alice in the house would bring bad memories. His wife is expecting a baby, and she's twenty years older than Alice's mother was when she gave birth to Alice. That would worry anyone. But Uncle Will said *more* than that.

And now this ghost . . . there are too many parallels for my peace of mind.

Why does the presence of a ghost make "too many parallels" to that long-ago tragedy?

My fingers travel across the bindings of the ledgers until I reach the 1880 census. Flipping to the *R*s, I find Grandmother Roosevelt's family and the address of her home, 6 West Fifty-Seventh Street. Then I switch to the most recent copy of the New York City Supernatural Registry, which lists every house in the city that's ever been haunted (back to 1822, when the registry was founded) and when each ghost faded into oblivion, assuming it ever did.

I am not entirely surprised to find 6 West Fifty-Seventh Street listed in the registry, although it's a bit of a shock to see my suspicion spelled out in print. Does Alice know this? I can't imagine her keeping it a secret if she did. I copy it down, then take my notes and go looking for Mrs. Adams.

Aunt Bye is out visiting a sick friend when I arrive at her house, and Uncle Will is at the navy yard in Brooklyn, so

Maisie sends me upstairs to Alice. I expect her to be in the attic, but I find her in her bedroom.

She whirls around when I knock on her half-open door, looking ready to jump out of her skin. "Eleanor, what are you doing here?"

"I have the information you wanted from the library." I look her up and down. Dust and cobwebs adhere to her skirt and blouse. Her nose is red, and her eyes are puffy. "I guess you searched the attic?"

"Until it got too cold. I didn't expect to see you so soon." She scowls as if I'm the last person she wants to talk to. This is typical Alice. She sent a letter asking for my help, and now she's annoyed at me for providing that help.

Aggravation flares inside me, and I march into her room, brandishing my library notes in her face. "In 1830, a Mr. Edgar Drummond lived in this house with his wife, three children, and a housemaid. Ten years later, the first Mrs. Drummond must have died because there's a new wife listed in the census, and she had two children of her own plus a new baby with Mr. Drummond. The eldest Drummond son also had a wife and baby living here. There were *ten* people in the house that year—six of them under the age of sixteen. But by 1850, only the second Mrs. Drummond and her youngest son, David, were left. Maybe the others grew up and moved away—but one or more of them may have died. I think we have several candidates for the ghost's progenitor."

At the beginning of my speech, Alice stands stiffly, arms crossed. But when I start talking about the children, her demeanor loosens. Dashing one hand across her eyes, she holds out her hand for the notes. While she reads the list of names and ages, I cast a surreptitious look at her face. Has she been crying? Alice?

"We can eliminate the girls," she says, pointing to *Susannah Drummond* and her stepsister, *Mary Isabel Brown*. "And the older boys. We're looking for a boy between ten and thirteen, I'd say."

"How do you know?"

"I saw him."

My mouth falls open. "The ghost?"

"His shadow, anyway."

I take another look at Alice, head to toe. "Did it frighten you?"

"No!" she exclaims indignantly, her cheeks burning red. "Of course not! But while it was there, the temperature dropped to arctic levels, and I had to come downstairs to warm up."

She's lying. Something happened to Alice in the attic that left her shaken like a bottle of soda water about to fizz over. I can't imagine what that could be—especially from a Friendly ghost who makes tea for visitors—but when Alice shuffles my notes to look at the last page, I worry about how she will react and grab the paper to stop her.

Alice gapes at me. It's too late to hide this information from her; she's about two seconds from ripping the sheet of paper out of my hands. But maybe I can prepare her for the blow. "What do you know about the house you were born in?"

"The house I was born in? What do you mean?"

"Your parents were living with our grandmother, Martha Roosevelt, at the time you were born."

"I know that."

"The house was Number Six on West Fifty-Seventh Street. According to the city registry, that house was declared Unsafe for Habitation after the outbreak of a Vengeful in February 1884, and the designation hasn't been changed since." I don't have to remind Alice that February of 1884 is the month she was born, and the month her mother and our grandmother died. I remove my hand and let her read my notes for herself.

The blush drains from her cheeks, leaving her skin the color of porcelain. "Who is the progenitor of this . . . Vengeful?"

"That's not listed in the public records."

I checked with the librarian. Information on progenitors is protected by privacy law. Nobody wants strangers knowing that their great-aunt Minnie erupted as a Vengeful and killed seven people. You can petition the Supernatural Registry board if you're the owner of a haunted house or potentially buying one, and if the progenitor's name is recorded, they'll tell you. But they won't hand that information over to anyone else. "Your father and Aunt Bye were there when it happened," I remind Alice, "and your father now owns the house. If anyone knows, they do."

She stares at the paper for a long, long time, then abruptly opens a drawer in her dresser. Pushing aside bloomers and petticoats, she fishes out a handful of bills. It's more money than she should have as a spending allowance, and I'm alarmed to watch her stuff the bills into her skirt pocket. "What are you doing?" I ask, even though I can guess, especially when Alice pins on that hat with the ridiculous ostrich feathers.

"I want to see it for myself." She pulls her blue coat out of her wardrobe.

"What? How are you going to get there?"

Alice sweeps out of the room without responding, and I chase after her, leaving my notes behind.

Census Records for 132 East 21st Street

1830
Edgar Drummond—Head of Household—38
Amelia Drummond—Wife—30
Edgar Drummond, Jr.—Son—10
Benjamin Drummond—Son—5
Susannah Drummond—Daughter—2
Betty Piper—Housemaid—14

1840
Edgar Drummond—Head of Household—48
Ella Drummond—Wife—32 (must be second wife)
Edgar Drummond, Jr.—Son—20
Lisandra Taylor Drummond—
    Daughter-in-law—19
Edgar Drummond, the 3rd—Grandson—1
Benjamin Drummond—Son—15
Susannah Drummond—Daughter—12
Charles Brown—Stepson—10
   (Ella's from first marriage?)
Mary Isabel Brown—Stepdaughter—9
David Drummond—Son—1
    (Edgar & Ella's son, probably)

1850

Ella Drummond—Head of Household—42

David Drummond—son—11

(I assume Mr. Drummond died.

   Where did all the other family members go?)

New York City Supernatural Registry

6 West 57th Street

Roosevelt Household

Owned at the time of eruption by

   Martha Bulloch Roosevelt

Designated Unsafe for Habitation, February 1884

Haunting Type—Vengeful

Designation never changed!

Current owner—Theodore Roosevelt, Jr.—

   Uncle Teddy!

9

ELEANOR ON AN ESCAPADE

I follow Alice out to the street, where she raises her arm in an attempt to summon a hansom cab. Two pass without stopping.

"Alice, wait!" I exclaim.

"Why won't these cabs stop for me?" She waves a dollar bill over her head as proof of her ability to pay.

"Because none of them want to pick up two girls without a chaperone." I hardly believe I'm including myself in Alice's escapade, but I cannot let her run off alone in her current state of distress.

Alice looks me up and down. "*You* could be the chaperone. You're tall enough. Take off that horrible bonnet and coat."

"What?" Alice is already untying my bonnet, tugging it from my head. She pulls pins from her own hair and uses them to coil my braid under the ostrich monstrosity. We switch outer garments. Alice swims in my brown wool coat, while I can barely force my shoulders into her fashionable tailored one.

But she's right. Within seconds of my recostuming, a hansom cab stops for us. The cabman shoots me a doubtful glance when he gets a better look at my face. Then Alice holds up her bill again and he waves us into the carriage. "Number Six West Fifty-Seventh Street," Alice says. The driver clucks to his horse, pretending we are an ordinary fare and not two girls who shouldn't be gallivanting around the city on our own.

Alice's lips are pinched, and her leg jiggles in a very unladylike way. "What made you look up my grandmother's house in the supernatural registry?"

Our grandmother's house, I want to remind her. Instead, I consider how to answer. I may not like Alice very much, but I'm not cruel enough to wound her with the knowledge that Uncle Will regrets welcoming her to his home. "It was a comment Grandmother Hall made," I tell her, and she nods because that is believable.

Which makes me wonder, belatedly, why I've never heard a whisper of gossip from Grandmother Hall about my grandmother Roosevelt's house being haunted by a Vengeful. Perhaps, just this once, she kept the story to herself out of respect for my relatives.

The ride takes a quarter of an hour, and the cab stops on a street filled with majestic homes three times the size of my own. My eyes jump immediately to the sign nailed to the door of Number 6—faded black letters on a faded yellow background, but still readable.

UNSAFE FOR HABITATION

The driver of the cab sees it too and opens his mouth to say something, but Alice offers him his fare and an overly generous tip. The man takes it, clamps his lips shut, and signals his horse to move on. I feel abandoned, especially when Alice leaves my side and strides purposefully toward that house.

"Alice! Don't get too close!"

"The ghost is *inside*," she calls back. "It's not going to come out and get us."

Once again, I find myself following her like a child's toy on a string.

From the outside, the house looks similar to the others on this street: multiple stories in tawny stone with tall windows, balconies, and sloping rooflines. But something emanates from Number 6 that makes my heart race. The street is unnaturally still for the middle of the day, especially in a neighborhood this close to Central Park. It's as if everybody knows to avoid this block.

"Eleanor, come look." Alice climbs onto the iron streetside fence, trying to peer through one of the first-floor windows.

My skin crawls, but I approach, one grudging step at a

time. Waves of cold roll from the house, like a fireplace that throws off ice instead of flames. The draperies on this front window are open, surprisingly, but there's a thick layer of frost on the *inside* of the glass.

"There's furniture inside," Alice says.

"How can you tell?"

"I can see the shapes—dimly. That's a grandfather clock next to a sofa, maybe."

"What are you girls doing?"

We both jump. Alice nearly tumbles over the fence, but I grab her by the belt of her coat and haul her back. Then we face the woman who's scowling at us from the threshold of the house next door. "Get away from there," she snaps. "That house is Unsafe."

"Yes, we know—" I begin.

"This house belongs to my father," Alice interrupts. "I was born here."

The woman tips her head to scrutinize us. She's perhaps fifty, thin as a poker with a face like a hatchet. "You're a Roosevelt?" Alice nods. "You'd better come in."

Alice and I look at each other. A neighbor who knows our family and the history of Number 6? We collide in our haste to scurry down the sidewalk and up the steps to the front door of her home. She waves us inside and closes the door.

The entrance hall is wide and high-ceilinged. There's a second-floor landing overlooking the foyer, accessible by two curved marble staircases. The woman leads us directly into a grand front parlor that could swallow several rooms in Grandmother's house. "Take off your coats and hats, girls. I'll bring in tea."

"Oh, thank you," I say. "But you don't have to—"

"It's already made." Before I can protest again, the woman darts from the room. I wonder if she's going to deliver instructions to a servant, because in a house this large, I expect she must have servants.

Alice unties my old bonnet, and I remove the ostrich hat, but neither of us takes off our coat. The room is too cold, the small fire in the corner fireplace too weak to hold off the chill of winter. Or, perhaps, the chill of the house next door.

"Maybe we shouldn't have come in here," I whisper. I've never been in a stranger's house except in the company of an adult, and this house seems *odd*. It reminds me of Aunt Bye's front hallway on the day after the eruption. Shadows are long and deep and . . . somehow . . . too many.

Alice jumps in her seat and jerks around to look at the wall behind her, the wall that neighbors her father's house. I don't know what caught her attention, but when I peer across the gloom I notice that the wallpaper on that wall is different from the rest of the room. At first I think it's a different pattern. Then I realize it's the same paper except blackened by mildew.

The woman returns carrying a heavy tray, which she sets down on the low table in front of our chairs. "I'm Miss Barnstable," she says. I glance at the door, but there's no sign of a maidservant.

"I'm Alice Roosevelt," my cousin says.

Miss Barnstable gives her a sharp look. "I forgot they named you after your mother."

Alice stares at her eagerly. "You lived here then?"

"I've lived here all my life. I went to school with your aunt Bye."

That surprises me. She looks ten years older than Bye. "I'm Eleanor, Elliott's daughter."

Miss Barnstable nods briefly at me, but her attention seems fixed on Alice as she pours tea into our cups. "I can't believe it's been so long."

"Can you tell us what happened?" I ask. Alice shoots me an angry look.

Miss Barnstable places a plate of cheese on the table. "You don't know?"

"Of course we know," Alice says, glaring at me. "But there are so many false rumors. I want to make sure people know what really happened."

"I'll fetch the cake." Miss Barnstable straightens.

"Please don't go to any trouble. Tea and cheese is generous enough." Alice reaches for a chunk and stops. The cheese is hard, cracked, and yellow, as if it was sliced days ago and left out. She withdraws her hand.

"I'll be right back," our hostess chirps.

"Thank you, but—" She ignores me entirely and disappears into the back of her house. I turn on Alice. "Why are you glaring at me like that?"

"You can't let her know our family didn't tell us what happened or she won't tell us either. Adults stick together. We have to pretend she's confirming what we already know." Alice whips around and looks at the wall again. "Do you hear that?"

"Hear what?" The only sound in the room besides our voices is the crackle of wood burning in the fireplace.

"Nothing." She faces forward again, but her leg bounces up and down.

"Alice?"

"Leave it be, Eleanor."

What is she not telling me? I pick up my teacup purely for the warmth, but when I look at the contents, my hand flinches, sloshing liquid over the rim.

The surface of the tea is slick and oily.

"Here we are," Miss Barnstable sings out, returning with a cake plate. She almost catches me pouring my tea back into the pot. "It's German chocolate cake. My favorite."

I eye it warily, but this offering looks edible: three layers, iced with a coconut-laden frosting. She slices into the cake, cutting a wedge, which she lays on a separate serving plate.

Worms ooze from the center of the cake—long, gray, dead, cooked worms.

I jump to my feet, and Miss Barnstable smiles at me, her teeth too shiny and a little too sharp. She holds out the plate full of cake and worms. I back away and grab Alice by the arm, yanking her to her feet. "We're leaving!"

Alice resists. "But she hasn't told us—"

"She isn't going to tell us anything!" I try to pull Alice away from the table, but she lunges back. To my horror, I think she's reaching for that slice of cake. But no, it's her feathered hat that she snatches from the arm of my chair.

Then the two of us flee the house, running hand in hand.

10

ALICE LEARNS THE TRUTH

LICE lets Eleanor drag her two blocks before digging in her heels. Eleanor, with those coltish legs, could probably keep going a mile before getting winded. But Alice needs to catch her breath. "What is *wrong* with that woman? Is she completely off her trolley? She baked *worms* in her cake!"

Eleanor's eyes are wide with shock. "She's like Miss Havisham!"

"Who?" Alice recognizes the name a second after asking the question but doesn't stop Eleanor from launching into an explanation of the jilted bride from *Great Expectations* who goes mad living close to a powerful Vengeful ghost. She needs that minute of Eleanor prattling to recover her wits.

Eleanor didn't hear the voice. That crazy woman didn't hear it. Only I did.

It sounded like a tree branch scraping against window shutters, scritching and scratching.

Al—ice. Al—ice. Come hoooommme.

"Alice, are you listening to me?"

"Yes!" Alice shoves her hat at her cousin. "Here. Put this on and get us a ride home."

Eleanor takes the hat but looks around. "Where's my bonnet? Did it get left behind?"

"Yes. I did you a favor."

Their ruse doesn't work a second time. No matter how imperiously Eleanor waves, no cab will stop for her. Eventually, they resign themselves to walking the hour or so back to Bye's house. "Take the hat back," Eleanor says after half an hour. "Your ears are bright red, Alice."

"I can't wear that hat with this coat. Are you mad?"

"Take them both back. The coat doesn't fit me anyway."

"Fine!" Right there on the street, under the curious looks of bystanders, she and Eleanor swap coats. Alice gets her hat back, already warmed by Eleanor's head, which comforts her stinging ears. They continue walking.

"That poor woman," Eleanor says. "Where's her family? Why do they let her live in that house?"

"Maybe she doesn't have anyone."

"That's terrible. Somebody should help her."

Alice shrugs. Miss Barnstable is not their problem.

Eleanor doesn't try to make conversation again, and Alice's thoughts swirl during their cold forty-block walk. By the time they get home, her hands are frozen and her feet are blistered. When she learns from Maisie that Aunt Bye has returned from visiting, Alice bursts into the parlor with Eleanor trailing behind.

Aunt Bye is reading a newspaper but looks up when they enter. "Girls! Maisie told me you went out. Where—"

"We went to Number Six, West Fifty-Seventh Street," Alice says.

Aunt Bye flinches, and the newspaper drops into her lap. "Why—"

"Eleanor found out at the library. We went and looked at the house." Alice marches across the room. "Did a Vengeful ghost kill my mother?"

"No!" Aunt Bye takes her niece's hands and pulls her down on the sofa. "Oh, Alice, your hands are blocks of ice! No, a ghost did not kill your mother."

Alice's relief is tempered by another, more difficult-to-name emotion. Because as horrifying as it would be to learn that a Vengeful murdered her mother, such a revelation would also liberate her from a lifelong burden. "Was it me, then? I killed her, by being born?"

"No, Alice, you did not. Didn't your father tell you what happened?"

"Father never speaks of her." Alice doesn't bother to disguise the bitterness in her voice. "It's as if she never existed. I know he wishes *I* didn't."

Across the room, Eleanor sucks in her breath, and Aunt Bye squeezes Alice's hands. "That isn't true! Your father adores you, and he loved your mother dearly. He should have explained to you years ago that your mother died of a kidney disorder. She wasn't diagnosed with the disease until well into her pregnancy, and there is no treatment for it in any case. It was lucky she was able to deliver you safely, as sick as she was."

Alice's eyes sting. She glances across the room at Eleanor, who casts her gaze at the floor, giving her cousin privacy without leaving the room. To her surprise, Alice isn't annoyed that she's still here. If it weren't for Eleanor, Alice would still know nothing about the events surrounding her birth. "What about my grandmother? How did she die?"

Aunt Bye closes her eyes. This is *her* mother they're talking about, and Alice is sorry to cause her pain. But now that the subject is open, she intends to find out everything she can. "Typhoid fever," Aunt Bye says. "We kept her isolated from your mother to avoid contamination, and we *thought* Mother was going to recover. But she took a turn for the worse." Only then does Aunt Bye open her eyes. "The end was very sudden, and no one was expecting it."

No one is expecting the sudden flash of white near the ceiling either. Aunt Bye stiffens, Eleanor squeaks, and Alice gapes as a handkerchief floats gently through the air and onto the sofa. "Thank you." Aunt Bye's voice rises at the end, as if it's a question rather than a statement. She picks up the handkerchief and unfolds it slowly, making sure it's nothing more than what it seems.

"What about the ghost?" Alice asks. "The Vengeful, I mean. Not this one."

Aunt Bye dabs at her eyes. "The eruption caught us by surprise while we were grieving."

When she doesn't offer any other information, Eleanor asks, "Who was the ghost's progenitor?"

"We don't know. We evacuated the house and never went back."

Eleanor makes a small noise, as if starting to say something and then changing her mind. It's Alice who continues the questioning. "That ghost is really strong. Why wasn't anything done to fade it? It doesn't look like the furniture was even removed!"

"It's dangerous to go in there, Alice."

"That's why there are specialists." Watching her pregnant aunt cringe, Alice feels a twinge of guilt, but there's something about this conversation that reminds her of a fish wriggling on a hook. She's not about to stop reeling it in.

"It's expensive to empty an Unsafe house. Your father was a widower, with an infant child, and unexpectedly burdened with our family finances. He decided to wait out the haunting. I know that house is worth hundreds of thousands of dollars, and he's waited far too long. But your father is stubborn. You know that."

Alice does know that. It's a trait he passed to all his children.

"Even an empty house doesn't guarantee the quick fading of a ghost," Aunt Bye goes on. "An alternative is selling the property to a developer who will tear the house down and rebuild. But that's our childhood home, Alice. We don't want to see it razed."

Alice understands. It's why she doesn't want Aunt Bye to abandon this house and rent another. *This* brownstone is *Alice's* childhood home.

Nevertheless, the explanation bothers her. Her father and her aunts don't want the house torn down, but they don't mind seeing it rot under the influence of a Vengeful? Alice looks across the room at Eleanor, and her cousin stares back, trying to telegraph a message. Alice has no idea what it is.

Her hesitation creates a hole, which Eleanor jumps in to fill. "Thank you, Aunt Bye. We feel so much better, knowing the truth. It must've been a horrible time for you, and I'm sorry if we've made you relive it."

"Darlings," Aunt Bye says, squeezing Alice's hands and gazing across the room at Eleanor. "Don't be sorry. I'm sorry you imagined the worst. The truth is terrible enough, and I've had a horror of ghosts ever since. The one in *this* house gives me the chills even when it does something kind."

She indicates the handkerchief, but Alice isn't convinced that was meant as a kind gesture. On the surface it seems so, but when the handkerchief first fell from the ceiling, Alice had the distinct impression that the ghost was mocking her aunt's tears.

"I'm going to have a lie-down before afternoon tea." Aunt Bye pushes off the arm of the sofa to stand and presses one hand to the small of her back. "Eleanor, will you stay and join us?"

"Thank you, but Grandmother will be looking for me." After Aunt Bye kisses her and leaves the room, Eleanor strides directly to the sofa like a girl with something on her mind and sits down next to Alice. "I don't think she was telling us the whole truth. You know who else died in that house? Years before we were born?"

Alice nods slowly. "Our grandfather. You think he's the progenitor of the Vengeful?"

"It would explain why they've never mentioned the ghost. And why they left the house untouched. They don't want his reputation tarnished. I think they kept the whole thing as quiet as possible and sacrificed the house and everything in it to keep the secret safe."

That scritch-scratch voice Alice heard, calling to her through Miss Barnstable's wall—was it her own grandfather, taunting her?

"Alice, what did you hear in Miss Barnstable's house that I didn't?"

Eleanor's clear blue eyes fix worriedly on Alice's face. It occurs to Alice that her cousin might read her far better than Alice can read Eleanor. "In that house? It was probably mice in the walls. Or snakes."

Eleanor sighs in exactly the same way Mother Edith does when she knows Alice is lying.

U.S.S. *MAINE* EXPLODES
IN HAVANA HARBOR

OVER 200 OF HER CREW MISSING, PRESUMED LOST

TREACHERY, ACCIDENT, OR SUPERNATURAL AGENCY?

Havana, February 16, 1898—At quarter to ten o'clock last evening, a terrible explosion took place on board the United States battleship *Maine* in Havana Harbor. Many of the crew were killed or wounded, with over 200 men still unaccounted for.

The explosion shook the whole city, breaking windows in houses.

An Associated Press correspondent who interviewed surviving sailors reports that they cannot account for the cause, having been asleep at the time of the explosion. An investigation is underway to determine whether the tragedy on the warship was the result of accident, supernatural agency in the form of a Vengeful, or an act of foreign treachery.

SEÑOR DE LÔME

Señor de Lôme, the Ambassador of Spain to the United States, said that there was no possibility that the Spaniards had anything to do with the destruction of the *Maine*. "The explosion must have been caused by an accident on board the warship or perhaps by a ghost."

THE MAINE'S VISIT TO HAVANA

The *Maine* sailed to Havana on Jan. 24, and was the first American warship to visit that port since the outbreak of the Cuban rebellion against Spain. Its presence signaled the continued trade between the U.S. and Cuba, despite outside hostilities.

The *Maine* was commanded by Capt. Charles D. Sigsbee, who was injured in the explosion but is expected to survive along with several other officers. The enlisted men sleeping in the forward part of the ship and those on late-night duty took the brunt of the blast and are primarily among the missing and dead.

Reports of a Vengeful aboard the warship are rumored, but cannot be confirmed.

A Naval Court of Inquiry has been ordered, and the U.S. Department of Ghost Diagnosticians is sending representatives to consult with the Cuban diagnosticians already on the scene.

President McKinley has committed "whatever resources necessary" to investigate and resolve the incident.

11

ELEANOR DEFIANT

*T*HIS morning is the day I speak to Grandmother about my schooling. I'm inspired by Alice, I think, and the way she charged across Manhattan to confront her family secrets. By comparison, I've been dawdling and delaying, waiting for the perfect moment to have the conversation and finding excuses to not even try.

After looking through my clipped editorials and newspaper articles, I decide not to complicate matters by debating the *merits* of female education. All Grandmother cares about is the money and the logistics. To counter that, I will present my three schools in a planned strategy: Allenswood, Linden, and then Wadleigh.

Breakfast is toast and tea, as always. Grandmother raises her eyes to me when I join her at the table. "You're looking flushed. Are you unwell? You should put yourself back into bed, and I will send Rosie upstairs with a tonic."

I shudder. Grandmother's tonics are bitter and oily and make me claim immediate improvement solely to ward off a second dose. Which may very well be their purpose. "I'm not unwell. I have a matter I wish to discuss with you."

Her eyebrows rise, but she does not stop buttering her toast. "What matter has you in such a state, then?"

"I want to continue my education."

"We have already spoken about this, Eleanor."

"I intend to speak about it again." *I intend* pops out of my mouth instead of *I wish* or *I'd like*, and for a moment I tremble, thinking Alice has influenced me too much. But Grandmother does not interrupt, so I continue. "I have looked into a number of schools, and my favorite is the Allenswood Academy in London. The headmistress, Madame Souvestre, has an excellent reputation."

"A school in London, run by a Frenchwoman. I suppose you'd like me to buy you a Swiss castle while I'm at it? What are you thinking, Eleanor? Have you discovered Bluebeard's treasure in the basement? The travel costs alone would send me to the poorhouse." Grandmother launches into a litany of the *obstacles to* and *dangers of* traveling abroad. She lingers on the likelihood of an ocean disaster because she knows I have never gotten over the terror of being lowered into a lifeboat with my parents after the S.S. *Britannic* collided with another vessel when I was not quite three years old.

I wait until she takes a breath and proceed as planned. I never expected her to agree to Allenswood. I am merely herding her in the right direction. "Another excellent option is Linden Hall in central Pennsylvania. No ocean crossing required."

"I've heard of that one," Grandmother snaps. "Run by Moravians. I would be a poor guardian indeed if I sent you to the wilds of Pennsylvania to be schooled by an obscure religious sect."

The Moravians have been educating girls at Linden Hall since the 1700s, which seems highly commendable to me.

"Your duty is here, Eleanor." Grandmother raps her knuckles on the table. "To me. I took in your family when you had nowhere else to go and accepted the burden of guardianship for you and your brother after the lamentable deaths of your parents. The least you could do in return is attend your grandmother in her old age and infirmity."

Infirmity? Grandmother is as sturdy as those ocean liners she claims sink with regularity. "Then you will like my third choice," I tell her. "Last year, the New York City School Board authorized the founding of a high school for girls, the Wadleigh School. The city will be constructing a new school building for it only a few blocks from here." It's more like a hundred blocks, but I'll break that news later. "Tuition would be minimal or free, but most importantly, I can live here." She shakes her head while I'm talking, but I press on. "Grandmother, it is ideal. I can take classes *and* stay here with you, at almost no cost."

"They're not going to build that school," she says.

"They are. It was voted on and approved."

"Then it will be unapproved. *No one* is going to waste

resources building a high school for girls when the country is at war."

I stare at her blankly for a few seconds. "What do you mean?"

"Have you not read this morning's newspaper?"

My eyes travel to the folded paper beside her elbow on the table. "You know I haven't." Is that Alice coming out of my mouth again?

A gleam lights her eyes as she hands me the newspaper. I scan the headlines first, and the words *explosion*, *treachery*, *missing*, and *dead* jump out at me. My heart turns to stone and drops into my stomach while I read the whole article carefully. "It may not have been an attack by Spain," I say hoarsely. "It could've been a Vengeful. Or a gas explosion."

Grandmother flattens out her lips. "It will be neither of those if war is more profitable. Mark my words. Your uncle will go to Cuba, of course."

At first I think she means Alice's father, but then I realize she's referring to Uncle Will. "No," I whisper. He can't go. Aunt Bye is expectng a baby. They have a ghost in the house.

How can I have been so selfish, thinking about my own ambitions this morning, while my aunt's world was falling into a deep, dark pit?

"A shame," Grandmother says, but there's satisfaction in her expression, as if she's already imagining my aunt as a war widow.

I stand. "I have to go to Aunt Bye."

"Absolutely not. They have enough to deal with. I will not add you to their burden."

I am always a burden. A burden to her. But also a burden to anyone who takes me away from her. Lips trembling, I repeat myself. "I am going to Aunt Bye's." Then I turn on my heel and walk out of the room.

"Eleanor! Come back here at once!"

I hear her rising from her chair. Does she mean to try to stop me? I grab my coat and dart out the front door before she makes it into the hallway.

Slamming the door behind me, I rage silently at my mother for leaving my father all those years ago and bringing us here to live. And at my father for giving her cause. From there, my thoughts unravel. Should I also blame my mother for dying and taking my brother Elliott with her? Surely my father deserves a share of my anger. He left us in Grandmother's care after their deaths, too caught up in his own grief to consider ours.

Stopping on a street corner between my house and Aunt Bye's, I wipe my eyes. I defied Grandmother Hall once before, when I was nine. I still bear the marks from a hickory switch on the backs of my legs. Traffic pauses, and I surge across the street with the rest of the crowd, wondering if I would submit to such a punishment now. Tonight, if called on to do so, will I let her have at me? Or will I snatch the switch from her hand, toss it aside, and tell her, *No more*?

When I find myself in front of Aunt Bye's house, I push those questions aside. I can't go in if I'm more worried about

Grandmother than I am about my aunt. Taking deep breaths, I compose myself. Only then do I ring the bell.

The door opens, and Maisie exclaims, "Oh! Miss Eleanor! Isn't it terrible?"

I am whisked inside, my coat and bonnet taken by a whirlwind, and directed into the dining room, where *nobody* is eating their breakfast. The plate in front of Aunt Bye is empty, and Uncle Will's holds an intact congealed egg. Alice is there too, her face pinched, her plate pristine. Ida pours me tea, and I sit and stare across the table.

"Your uncle," Aunt Bye says to me, "is leaving for Cuba this morning."

"It is my duty to go," Uncle Will replies, not to me but to his wife. "If the explosion was caused by an accident or a ghost, I'll be home in a few days."

"Yes," Aunt Bye agrees woodenly.

Uncle Will puts his hand over hers. "You'll be well taken care of while I'm gone. The solicitor is going to send a list of potential houses to rent. You can visit them and decide which suits you best, and by the time you've made up your mind, I'll be back to help with the move. In the meantime, Alice will keep you company, and Eleanor—" He looks at me. "You'll visit every day, won't you?"

"Yes, of course," I say, thinking I might need to *live* here if Grandmother throws me out for my disobedience. But I doubt she will let go of me that easily.

"The cousins are still coming tomorrow, aren't they?" Alice asks.

Aunt Bye puts her fingertips to her mouth. "Perhaps I should cancel their visit."

"Don't," Uncle Will says. "It will be better to have young people around, keeping your spirits up. And speaking of spirits, *I'll* feel better knowing you have a strapping lad like Franklin here to handle incidents such as this morning."

I glance around the table. "What happened this morning?"

"The ghost stacked all the chairs on the dining room table."

"Like a puzzle," Alice adds, intertwining her fingers. "With the legs tangled together."

Uncle Will grunts in agreement. "Took me a few minutes to disassemble them without the whole structure crashing to the ground."

"Is that normal?" In books, Friendlies are helpful and charming, like invisible servants. This ghost did something in the attic to make Alice cry.

"Apparently, our ghost is a mischief-maker." Uncle Will looks worriedly at his wife. "Will you be all right, Bye? Tell me if you will not, and I will telegraph my superior and say I cannot come."

I hold my breath. What Uncle Will is offering to do is *not done*. A soldier doesn't decline an order from his superior. For an officer of Uncle Will's rank, it could mean the end of his career.

Aunt Bye knows this too. "No, Will. You can't do that." She clasps his hands tightly. "You *will* be home before the baby is born?"

"Long before he is born, my darling."

"Or she," Aunt Bye reminds him, her eyes shining.

"Or she," he agrees, leaning close to her.

I enjoy a good literary romance—the novels *Pride and Prejudice* and *Sense and Sensibility* are favorites of mine—but there is something about seeing it in person, between people of a certain age, who are *related to you*, that makes the whole thing embarrassing. I look at Alice. She flings her napkin to the table, and we flee the dining room before Aunt Bye and Uncle Will start canoodling right in front of us.

"Your father won't have to go to Cuba, will he?" I ask after we escape into the hallway.

"His job as assistant secretary of the navy will require that he stay in Washington," Alice says with just enough tartness in her voice for me to stare at her, not taking that as a full answer. After a moment, she exhales in exasperation. "But you don't know my father very well if you think he'll stay behind while everyone's attention is on Cuba. If he could, Father would be the corpse at every funeral, the bride at every wedding, and the baby at every christening."

I want to protest her harshness, but I'm not sure she's wrong. Before I can say anything, Uncle Will exits the dining room and strides toward us. "Girls, I am counting on you to look after Bye."

"Of course," Alice replies, sounding offended he would think otherwise.

"No more sudden excursions." His voice takes on an uncharacteristic sternness. "I mean it. I understand that you were curious, but you dredged up painful memories and emotions, which are difficult in her present state."

Tears spring to my eyes. "I'm sorry." It was my fault. I was the one who eavesdropped on a conversation not meant for me and pursued it in the library files. I drove Alice to that house.

"I'm sorry too," Alice says, and I whip around to stare at her because I don't think I've ever heard her say those words before. "What should we do about the ghost?"

Uncle Will glances around as if the ghost might be lurking in the billiards room or peeping over the banister. "It won't hurt to clear out the attic. But wait until your cousins arrive and get them to help you. Your aunt needs your full attention today. In fact, you should sit with her, eat breakfast, and convince her to eat too."

I have no appetite, but Aunt Bye needs to eat for the baby's sake, so I'll try.

The world has turned upside down since I woke this morning, convinced I'd have the better of Grandmother before the breakfast dishes were cleared away. But she has won. I can't pursue plans for my education in the midst of a national crisis. She might even be right about the Wadleigh School being canceled or postponed.

A ribbon of frigid air follows me and Alice as we make our way back to the dining room. A draft, perhaps. Or maybe the ghost is letting us know it's here and listening. For the time being, it too has won.

12

ELEANOR AND THE COUSINS

GRANDMOTHER chooses not to take the switch to me for my disobedience. I suspect she doesn't know whether I would submit, and neither do I, so it is just as well she doesn't test me. Instead, she gives me the cold shoulder.

One plate set for her evening meal.

One plate set for her breakfast.

If this is meant as a punishment, Grandmother has overestimated the pleasure of her own company. I eat with Rosie in the kitchen, listening to her stories about her grandchildren and feeling nothing but relief. Grandmother's silence means I don't need to tell her that I am leaving the house again after breakfast—or argue with her excuses for keeping me home.

By the time I reach Aunt Bye's the morning after Uncle Will's departure, my cousin Corinne has already arrived, having taken an early train from New Jersey. She's grown taller since she turned twelve but otherwise looks the same, with her cheerful round face and a huge bow on the back of her head restraining thick brown hair.

"Why do you never visit us in New Jersey ?" she asks, hugging me. "My brothers miss Gracie!"

"I'll try to do that this spring," I say, even though Grandmother won't allow me to travel with my six-year-old brother on my own, and she would never take us.

"Well, good! Because we see Alice more than we see you, and she lives farther away!"

Alice, who is perched on the arm of Aunt Bye's chair, casts her eyes down and makes no comment. Her stepmother and Corinne's mother have been close friends since childhood. I happen to know (because this is the kind of gossip Grandmother loves to tell) that Uncle Theodore met Edith through his sister when they were in their teen years and fell in love. Everyone thought they would get married, but unexpectedly, Uncle Theodore abandoned Edith for Alice Lee and married her instead. I once overheard Aunt Edith say that it was a lucky thing Aunt Alice died young because she would have bored Uncle Theodore to tears if their marriage had lasted longer. When Corinne's mother and Aunt Edith get together, they probably look at Alice as an embarrassing leftover from her father's mistake. I can't imagine those visits are comfortable for her.

The doorbell rings, and seconds later there is a great commotion in the hallway. The Hyde Park branch of the Roosevelt family has arrived.

Aunt Bye struggles to stand. Alice takes one arm to assist her, and Corinne slips under her other arm. "Do you have names picked out for the baby?" Corinne asks.

"William, if it's a boy. We haven't chosen a name for a girl."

Corinne's smile dimples both her cheeks. "I suggest you name her after your only sister and your favorite niece. Corinne!"

Aunt Bye smiles wanly. "Don't you think we have enough Corinnes in the family?"

"You can never have enough Corinnes."

Helen Roosevelt flies through the parlor door in a flurry of dark curls and feathers. She kisses Aunt Bye, then envelops Alice and Corinne in kisses while white downy tufts escape her swan-feathered wrap. When she turns to me, she gasps. "Eleanor, I almost didn't recognize you!" Helen bestows a feathery kiss on my cheek. "You've grown into an Amazon! Or, with that hair, maybe Boudica."

"Who?"

"Boudica." Helen winks. "Celtic queen. Slaughtered many Romans."

"That doesn't sound like our gentle Eleanor," Aunt Bye says with a laugh.

"Oh, I think Eleanor can be fierce if the occasion calls for it," says a voice from the doorway.

I didn't see Franklin come in behind Helen. "Hello," I say, my cheeks growing warm.

"Hello right back at you," Franklin replies with a smile.

I don't dare look in Alice's direction. *Once*, a long time ago, I told her I thought Franklin was the handsomest of the Roosevelt boys, and Alice assumes that means my affection for him is more than cousinly. Which isn't true.

Franklin and Helen are fifth cousins to me, once or twice removed—whatever that means. When I was younger, I assumed they were first cousins to each other, just like me and Alice and Corinne. Then I came to understand that Helen was the daughter of Franklin's much older half brother, which left me very confused. How could Franklin be Helen's uncle when they were almost the same age—and, in fact, Helen was the older of the two?

The answer is that the Roosevelt family tree is very complicated.

While Maisie collects hats and coats, Helen jokingly peeks behind the parlor curtains. "Where is this ghost I've heard about? Hiding?"

"Watching us," Alice says.

Helen gives a theatrical shudder. "Alice, you tease! Well, I have an idea I'm dying to try out. We should hold a séance. My friend Judith attended one at her cousin's house, and they were able to get a ghost to tell them its name."

"If we find out who the progenitor was, it's supposed to be easier to break its ties with the house," Franklin says. "You remove anything the progenitor might have a connection to."

"That's right," Helen agrees. "Judith gave me a pamphlet with instructions on how to do it properly, if everyone's game to try."

Franklin and Corinne chime in with enthusiasm. I look to see Alice's reaction. Since investigating the haunting with the "ghoal" of fading the ghost was her idea, I expect to see consternation over Helen taking charge of the plan. But Alice nods without comment, which is very unlike her.

I turn to see what Aunt Bye thinks, and that is when I realize she is no longer in the room. Which is as unlike Aunt Bye as subdued compliance is to Alice. Aunt Bye likes to be in the thick of things when the family is together. Walking out of the parlor, I head for the back of the house. She's likely in the kitchen, giving instructions to the servants or fetching a plate of freshly baked cookies. But I find only Ida and Maisie, preparing the midday meal. "Have you seen Aunt Bye?" I ask.

"Isn't she in the parlor?" asks Maisie.

I shake my head and take the servants' stairs because they're handy, even though I hate the enclosed stairwell. When I knock on Aunt Bye's bedroom door, she answers, "Come in." I discover her reclining in bed, fully dressed.

"Aunt Bye! Are you ill?"

"No, sweetheart. Just fatigued. I didn't sleep well last night."

Of course she didn't, not with her husband on a boat to Cuba. Today's newspaper had no new information on the explosion but plenty of editorials calling for a military response. I was shocked by the number of prominent citizens ready to declare war before the facts have even been discovered.

Downstairs, a doorbell rings. "Who can that be?" I wonder.

"Helen's friends," Aunt Bye says. "They've been sending calling cards all morning."

Helen always has a flock of friends wherever she goes, but . . . "Do they have to come today? It's her first day. She should spend time with *you*."

"Let her friends visit. I'm happy to host them." Aunt Bye's eyelashes flutter and close. She won't be hosting anyone this morning. When she begins to snore lightly, I cover her with a blanket and return to the kitchen.

Ida and Maisie look at me expectantly.

"She's taking a nap."

They must see the worry on my face because Ida says, "When my mother was carrying my youngest brother last year, she napped twice a day."

"The body knows what it needs," Maisie adds, sounding older and wiser than her years. She takes off her apron and picks up a basket. "I'm off to the market. We're having more people for today's dinner than expected and the grocery delivery is coming up short."

She sounds annoyed, and I am too. I wanted to spend time with my cousins, and now I have to share them.

Franklin and a couple of male visitors have congregated in what was formerly Aunt Bye's drawing room, now transformed by Uncle Will into a billiards room. In the front parlor, Helen holds court over half a dozen girls, their voices sounding like a cacophony of birds. Dressed in bright colors and rich fabrics, they all look very sophisticated and, to me, intimidating. I stop outside the doorway with no idea how to join them.

"What are you doing?"

I startle, hearing Alice's voice behind me. I'm not sure how to explain why I'm lurking in the hallway, but, glancing past me into the parlor, she seems to guess. "Go in and introduce yourself, Eleanor."

"I can't." Confessing this to Alice is a risk. I expect sharp words from her, but she surprises me.

"They can't make you feel awkward unless you let them. Sit down and join the conversation." Alice makes it sound easy, and for her, it would be. Before I can ask her to go in with me, she hurries away, calling back over her shoulder, "Franklin wants to meet Emily Spinach!"

Instead of entering the parlor, I return to the kitchen. If I find Fig Newtons or cake, I can offer refreshments to Helen's guests. It'll give me an excuse to go in and something to do with my hands. Looking around for a likely offering to put on a tray, I find instead a single blue teacup sitting in the middle of the kitchen table, with steam rising from the tea in it.

My blue teacup.

On the day my mother died, Aunt Bye took me and Gracie from Grandmother Hall's house and brought us here. Gracie was too young to know what was going on, but I understood. Our mother was gone forever, and our brother Elliott was not long for this world. Aunt Bye sat me down at this table and gave me tea in this blue cup. She told me it was a magical, one-of-a-kind teacup that would ease heartache. "Not today and not tomorrow. But every time you drink from it, your heart will hurt a little less."

Now I know it's only a mismatched teacup, the sole survivor of a set that no longer exists. But Aunt Bye still serves me with it whenever I take tea at her house.

I look around. Maisie has gone to the market, and Ida is nowhere to be seen. The kitchen is colder now than when I passed through minutes ago, which makes me think this tea is a gift from the ghost. "Thank you," I say to the empty room. I don't know if ghosts want thanks, but like Aunt Bye when that handkerchief floated down from thin air, I feel obligated. Reaching for the sugar bowl, I lift the lid—and recoil.

The sugar is hard and clumped, as if someone put a wet spoon into it. Worse, there are dead ants in the bowl. Remembering Miss Barnstable's worm cake, I shudder and cross the kitchen with the bowl, open the back door, and toss the contents outside.

Cold air rushes through the doorway, and strangely, it's rushing from the *inside* of the house to the *outside*, as if my opening the door has created a cross breeze. Riding the breeze is a girl's voice.

"Where's that cousin of yours who was galumphing around here earlier?"

I recognize Helen's voice when she answers. "Do you mean Franklin?"

"No, that great big girl with the long blond hair."

"Oh, that's Eleanor. I don't know where she is right now."

It's impossible to hear a conversation taking place in the front parlor while standing at the back of the house. And yet I can.

"Why does she dress like an orphan waif from the 1860s? Can't someone explain basic fashion sense to her? Or at least dispose of those horrible black stockings?"

Another voice chimes in. "I've seen her around the neighborhood, carrying books from the library. She's such an odd duck, like an old granny. You'd think she was eighty years old instead of fifteen!"

Odd duck. Granny. The room lurches. My mother used to call me those things.

"Eleanor is thirteen," I hear Corinne say. "Not fifteen."

"Thirteen? And already that tall? She'll be a giantess before she's through!"

Corinne laughs.

Sweet, funny, affectionate Corinne—who never let go of my hand at my brother's funeral—*laughs* at me.

The blow is so great, I double over. Then I plunge directly out the back door into the alley behind the house.

Without a coat, without a hat, I run home.

13

ALICE AT THE SÉANCE

*H*ELEN'S guests stay for the meal but leave shortly afterward—all except for a tall, round-faced fellow named George who seems besotted with Helen. When she declares her intention to hold a séance that very afternoon, George enthusiastically pledges his support.

So do Franklin and Corinne, which doesn't surprise Alice. Helen has always been their unofficial leader, and when she plans an activity, be it a game of charades, a scavenger hunt, a picnic, or a masquerade party, the Roosevelt cousins fall into line.

Opening up the pamphlet she got from her friend, Helen reads the pertinent parts aloud.

"Under NO circumstances attempt a séance with a Vengeful or an Aggressive Unaware. Even a harmless Unaware or Friendly may become agitated when given an opportunity to communicate with the living. Therefore, choose the venue carefully. Avoid confined spaces. A room with more than one exit is safest."

"The dining room is the obvious choice," Franklin says.

"It is wise to take precautions for the protection of the participants, such as a circle of iron or salt around the séance table."

"I'll handle that," George declares, then adds dotingly, "if that's agreeable to you, Helen."

"Not all ghosts are able to produce auditory phenomena, so provide an alternate means of communication, such as a talking board and a planchette or a pendulum."

"I have an idea." Franklin eyes the chandelier over the table.

"If you make a pendulum," Corinne says, "I can make the alphabet."

As her cousins size up the task, choose a role, and get right to it, Alice recognizes the influence of her father.

Every summer, Alice's father hosts the extended Roosevelt family at his estate on Oyster Bay, Long Island. One of their traditional excursions involves navigating the two-hundred-foot incline of Cooper Bluff to the beach. There are other beaches they could visit, but the appeal to Alice's father is the difficulty. He taught the cousins to work together in one long chain to descend the hill without losing their balance—not just the older ones, but also Corinne's little brothers and Alice's siblings. "We're Roosevelts!" her father loves to shout. "If one goes down, we all go down!"

Alice hates Cooper Bluff. *Hates it.* As bold as she likes

to think herself, she's not brave about feats of strength and coordination. Usually, while her cousins organize their chain by height and age, Alice complains bitterly, stamps her feet, and threatens not to go. Once, she really didn't go, and her father left her sitting at the top of the bluff. She spent that afternoon sweating in the sun while her cousins and siblings frolicked on the beach. After that, her refusals were empty threats, but being pulled down that hill as part of a chain of children has never ceased to terrify her.

Now she feels the same way. Watching her cousins prepare the dining room, Alice wants to stamp her feet and call a halt to this séance—and she doesn't know why. A chilled foreboding? The unexplained need to look behind her?

Alice hasn't been back to the attic since her first visit. She likes to blame that on the circumstances: the harrowing visit to her birthplace, followed by the tragedy in Cuba and Uncle Will's sudden departure. But the truth is, Alice has stood in the servants' staircase and stared up at the door to the attic three times in the past two days. And on every occasion the same words dropped into her head: *He must have wished you had never been born.*

Alice hasn't avoided the attic because she's afraid of the ghost. She has avoided the attic because she's afraid of what horrible truths the ghost might show her next.

Meanwhile, her cousins implement the first step in their plan to eliminate the haunting. Franklin detaches a crystal pendant from the chandelier above the dining table and rigs it to hang from a string, its point barely grazing the tabletop. Corinne writes the letters of the alphabet in a circle on a large sheet of butcher's paper and slides it under the pendant.

Helen and her admirer, George, collect every iron fire implement—poker, shovel, ash rake, and tongs—from every fireplace in the house. Together, they lay the tools on the floor around the dining table, each one crossing the ones adjacent to it so that the circle of iron is unbroken. To their dismay, they come up short. George rubs the back of his neck. "Well, I'll be . . ."

Helen holds up a finger and darts from the room, returning ten seconds later brandishing two cast-iron frying pans to close the distance. "This ought to do it."

Franklin frowns. "And this won't prevent the ghost from reaching the pendulum?"

"I don't know if it'll prevent the ghost from doing *anything*," Helen admits. "It's *supposed* to stop physical manifestations from reaching into the circle and"—she grabs Corinne by the shoulders, causing her to jump and scream—"throttling someone."

"Are we ready to start?" George asks.

Alice can see no reason to delay, despite her uneasiness. Aunt Bye has excused herself, wanting no part of it. She joined them at dinner and tried to appear cheerful for the sake of her guests, but Alice could tell she wasn't having a good day. Mother Edith had many similar days, especially in her last pregnancy.

With a sigh, Alice produces Eleanor's notes. "Eleanor thinks the progenitor is one of these children. *I* think it's one of the boys."

"Based on?" Helen prompts.

"Based on a shadow I saw in the attic."

"Oooh." Corinne clasps her hands together and squirms. "This is going to be spooky."

"Is Eleanor coming?" Franklin asks. "Should we wait for her?"

Alice hesitates. Eleanor left without telling anyone this morning, probably because she was too shy to meet Helen's friends. Alice could have introduced Eleanor to the group— *should have* introduced her. It would only have taken a few seconds of her time and would have been a kindness. But she didn't.

She also should have sent Eleanor a note telling her they were conducting the séance this afternoon. She *meant* to, but forgot.

"No," she tells Franklin. "Eleanor's not coming."

He shoves his hands in his pockets and nods, acknowledging her answer but not liking it. "Let's begin, then."

"Wait," says Corinne. "There's one more thing we need." She disappears for a minute and returns holding a pan full of ash from Aunt Bye's stove, which she pitches all over the dining table.

"Corinne!" Helen gasps.

"I read this in a book," Corinne explains. "If the pendulum moves, it'll leave a track in the soot as a record."

"That's a good idea," Alice says. "Except for the part where Maisie and Ida *kill you*."

"I'll clean up when we're done," Corinne promises.

"That's what you said when you and Teddy tried to make a sandbox in your mother's sun parlor," Alice reminds her. "How did that turn out?"

It had not turned out well. Franklin and Helen laugh at the memory, and Corinne sticks her tongue out at Alice.

There are two exits from the dining room—one to the hallway and one to the billiards room. Alice steps over the circle of iron and chooses a seat that provides an easy path to both doorways. One by one, her cousins and George select their own places and extend hands to one another.

Helen casts her eyes toward the ceiling like a preacher in church. "We are gathered here this afternoon to contact the ghost in this house," she intones solemnly. "We welcome communication with you. If you are here, give us a sign."

Corinne starts to giggle but stops abruptly as the air freezes around them. Everyone holds their breath in shock. Then Alice slowly exhales. Ice crystals hang in the air.

"You're here," Helen says, exhaling her own icy cloud. "Thank you for coming. Can you tell us your name?"

The pendulum remains motionless.

"Alice, read the names on your list."

Casting her eyes at Eleanor's precise handwriting, Alice picks out the names of the boys most likely to have died in this house as children: "Edgar Drummond. Charles Brown. David Drummond."

When the silence continues without a break, Helen calls out, "Are you one of those boys? Can you tell us your name?"

Glass tinkles. Alice jerks her gaze up to the chandelier, where the hanging crystals are rattling together. The pendant shivers on its string.

"Do you see it?" Corinne's whisper hangs in the air.

"See what?" Helen asks.

Corinne's head jerks left and right, the bow in her hair bobbing. "The shadow in the corner of your eyes."

Shivering, Alice glances around the room. At first, she sees nothing except the things she expects to be there. But when she holds herself completely still and concentrates on the periphery of her vision, the *extreme edge* of what she can see, she realizes there's another person in the room. Flitting among the shadows, hiding in the corners and edges and folds.

"Look at the pendulum," Franklin whispers.

Alice's attention snaps back to that crystal. It swings toward *D*, cutting a path through the soot, then toward A, followed by V and finally Y.

"Davy," Helen announces.

George asks, "How did you die?"

The temperature in the room drops even further, and Alice's teeth chatter.

With a glance toward Helen, George clears his throat and repeats his question in a more commanding tone. "How did you die?"

"We know its name," Franklin murmurs, frowning. "Perhaps we should end here."

"Don't be a goose, *Uncle Franklin*," Helen says. She calls him that when he tries to put a damper on her fun. "Let's find out what we can while we've got it here." She raises her voice. "The toys Alice found in the attic. Do any of them belong to you?"

Corinne shrieks. Everyone looks at her and then, following her gaze, at the center of the table. A few inches away from the pendulum lies a huge brown rat with an eight-inch naked tail. Its eyes are glassy, its feet splayed stiffly in the air.

The circle of hands stretches to a breaking point as people recoil and start to rise from their chairs. Tightening her grip on Corinne's and Franklin's hands, Alice calls out, "You like playing pranks, don't you, Davy?"

The entire room pauses.

"A snake in the attic," Alice continues. "A rat in the dining room. I bet you liked scaring your sisters." She glances at the list. "Susannah and Mary Isabel. Did you play tricks on them? I once put a toad on my sister's pillow. And my brother got blamed for it, which I consider killing two birds with one stone. Don't you?"

The dead rat vanishes. By the lack of indentations on the soot Corinne threw across the table, it was never *really* there. Everyone eases back into their seats.

"He likes you, Alice," Helen says. "*You* ask the questions."

Franklin shakes his head. "We have the information we need. We should stop."

"Davy," Alice says loudly—defiantly, because she's tired of this ghost getting the better of her, "what else do you want to tell us?"

Silence follows. Pressure builds in her ears, as if someone has stuffed cotton into them—and keeps stuffing and stuffing. The china in Aunt Bye's glass cupboard shudders. The crystals in the chandelier join the clamor, clanking together while the pendulum swings in a straight track across Corinne's alphabet circle.

T . . . T . . . T . . . T . . .

Alice's stomach cramps in a bout of sudden nausea. Across the table, Helen makes a retching sound and breaks the circle to clasp both hands over her mouth. George groans. Corinne pales.

"I'm ending this!" Franklin jumps out of his seat. He catches the pendulum in midswing and yanks on it, snapping the thread. "Everybody out of the room!"

He doesn't need to say it twice. They push back their chairs and rush for the doorways, kicking the iron safety circle out of the way. Alice ends up in the billiards room with Franklin and Corinne, while George follows Helen into the hallway.

Slowly, the chandelier stills, and the rattling inside the china cabinet ceases.

Alice places a hand on her stomach, but her nausea is gone as suddenly as it came.

Running a hand through his blond hair and leaving it disheveled, Franklin peers through the doorway across the dining room at George and Helen on the opposite threshold. "Told you we should've stopped after getting the name."

Davy Drummond.

Alice draws in a deep breath, wanting this ghost out of the house more than ever.

February 15, 1898

Darling Sissy,

Thank you for your lovely letter confirming your arrival at your aunt's house. It was so well written and sweet, I thought at first that Eleanor must have written it for you. I am happy to see your aunt's influence on your manners already.

Your brothers and sister miss you. Teddy is quite morose, although he has distracted himself by nursing an injured flying squirrel back to health. It seems our menagerie has expanded again, despite the subtraction of one snake.

I am wiring money to Bye for your dress expenditure. You need good clothes while you are there, and I would not have you looking as forlorn as Eleanor in her makeshifts.

Give my love to Bye and greetings to your uncle. Your father sends his love but is busy with work so you must not expect a letter from him, although you may write to him at any time for your letters always cheer him.

Fondly,
Mother Edith

February 15, 1898

Dear Sissy,

Washington is very boring without you. Even worse, with you gone, I get blamed for everything, even when it is not (entirely) my fault! For instance, Ethel is the one who broke Mama's cookie jar (after I convinced her to climb on my shoulders to reach it). But, unfairly, I was the only one punished.

Do you know what a rat king is? I read about it in a book. If you guessed "king of the rats," you are wrong. A rat king is a group of rats whose tails have become tangled together so badly that they cannot separate themselves. They live in a giant knot, which grows bigger every time another rat gets tangled with them.

I wish you were here because I am certain, if we were together, we could think of a way to make (or fake) a rat king and scare the maids. Plus, you would get the blame! Ha, ha, ha!

It is very unjust that you get to live in a house with a newly erupted Friendly ghost and I have to be stuck here in Washington. The little ones tattle too much. Mama fusses over the baby (who stinks), and Papa is at work all the time. I wish I were with you.

Your unfairly treated brother,
Teddy

Febuary 16, 1898

Dear ~~Elanor~~ Eleanor,

Thank you for your letter and for sending me the pikchure of you and me and Papa and Elliott. And the one of Mama. She was so pretty! I put them in my room so I feel like they are looking down on me from heven.

I made some freinds and am not so lonly no more. But sometimes I wish I could come home. Then I remember cold supper and no lights on til 7 and wish you were here with me insted.

Please send me more letters. And cake. The choclet kind.

Love,
Gracie

14

ELEANOR AND FRANKLIN

M Y punishment ends as quietly as it began. In the morning, when I find a breakfast plate set for me at the dining table, I take my seat and wish Grandmother good morning. She greets me as if nothing ever happened.

"I trust your cousins are well," she says, revealing, I think, the reason for my reprieve. She doesn't want to miss out on any Roosevelt family gossip.

She's going to be disappointed because I don't intend to spend much time with my cousins. Their visit is spoiled for me. I'll have to go back to Aunt Bye's at some point while they're here; otherwise Aunt Bye will press me for the reason why, and what happened was so humiliating I don't want to tell anyone. But I won't see them any more than I have to for common decency. Corinne laughed at me. Helen didn't speak a word in my defense.

How long have I been a subject of their jokes behind my back?

I thought that with *them*, I could be myself and not be judged for my lack of fashion and my awkward way of behaving. My heart aches with the loss of something I never had to define until it was taken away.

That afternoon, while I'm darning a pair of stockings in my room, Rosie sticks her head in the doorway. "You have a visitor, Miss Eleanor. He's in the front parlor with Mrs. Hall."

He? My mind goes to one particular person, but I make up my mind not to hope one way or another.

When I enter the parlor, it *is* Franklin sitting with Grandmother. "Yes," he's saying. "Father's health is precarious, and Mother is quite worried, as you would expect. Still, he tries to keep his spirits up."

"That is all one can do," Grandmother intones with an air of doom. Her eyes jump toward me. "Eleanor, your cousin Franklin is here."

"So I see." I hide my smile behind my hand, for when Grandmother turns in my direction, Franklin crosses his eyes. I believe that conveys his feelings about their conversation so far. I move to take a seat, but Franklin jumps to his feet.

"Mrs. Hall, with your permission, I'd like Eleanor to accompany me on a walk this afternoon."

My heart flutters in surprise.

"A walk?" Grandmother frowns. "Without a chaperone?"

Franklin tips his head and looks deliberately puzzled.

"Why, *I'll* be her chaperone, Mrs. Hall." Before Grandmother can adjust to that idea, he goes on. "A brisk walk is good for one's health. If my father were strong enough, I am sure that regular perambulation would restore his health in no time."

Grandmother's eyes dart between me and my cousin and finally settle on me. "It's up to you, Eleanor. If you go out with Franklin this afternoon, you won't have time to visit your aunt later. You have too many overdue chores here."

I nod, agreeing to her terms, and she dismisses us. Franklin accompanies me to the foyer and helps me on with my coat. "I'm sorry your father isn't well," I say gravely.

"Oh!" Franklin grins at me and lowers his voice. "Father's as well as he ever is. But I figured your grandmother would be more entertained by bad news than good."

I cover my smile, and the two of us begin our walk.

"It's a shame you weren't able to attend the séance yesterday," Franklin says.

I stumble, and he catches my elbow to steady me. I glance at him with mumbled thanks and look away to hide the flush in my cheeks. They held the séance without me? Without inviting me? Another pain lances through my heart because this is not just Corinne and Helen. It's *all* of them. "How did it go?" I ask because I must.

"The ghost gave us his name. Davy Drummond." He unfolds a paper from his pocket, and I recognize my census list. Franklin, or someone, has circled the name of David Drummond, who was eleven years old when he lived in the house with his mother in 1850.

Franklin recounts the details of the séance while I pretend that I don't care I wasn't included. His description fills me with both longing and revulsion. I'm relieved I wasn't subjected to the dead rat or the nausea, but I would've liked to see Franklin's clever pendulum and watch it spell out the ghost's name. "At the end," Franklin finishes, "the ghost became agitated when George and Alice pressed it with questions about its death."

"I don't think you're supposed to do that."

"I told them. But you know what Alice is like, and this George fellow was trying to impress Helen. Still, no harm done. Except that Corinne is in Maisie's bad graces because she isn't any better at cleaning up soot than sand!"

"Oh, the sandbox in the sun parlor! I forgot all about that." My aunt was so angry at Corinne and Teddy, and in truth I could hardly blame her. I lift my hand, and, to my surprise, Franklin captures my fingers in his own and swings our hands down to our sides.

"I wish you wouldn't do that. Cover your smile, I mean. I like your smile. It lights up your face."

My cheeks heat up, but at the same time, I can't keep the smile from spreading across them. I stare straight at the sidewalk between my feet until I realize he's stopped walking and we're standing outside a cemetery. Franklin tips his head at the gate. "I thought we could search for Davy's grave. Find out when he died."

I look through the iron bars. The stones jut from the ground at odd angles, like the snaggled teeth of an alley cat.

Or my teeth, for that matter. "You think he's buried here?"

"If the family lived in this neighborhood for over twenty years, this cemetery is the most likely place for them to be buried. This one or the one four blocks down."

He pushes open the gate. We enter side by side, but on the cemetery path, he lets go of my hand, and by silent agreement we walk in opposite directions, searching for the name Drummond.

Franklin spots the gravestones before I do. "Over here!"

I join him in standing before a pair of headstones, one for the father of the Drummond family, Edgar Senior, who died in 1842. He's buried beside his first wife, deceased eight years before him. Franklin points to the next row, and I see more familiar names. The oldest son, Edgar Junior, lies beside his young wife and their infant son. Lisandra and her baby died in 1841. Her husband died in 1844. Beyond these markers are even more Drummond graves.

The second son, Benjamin, died the same year as his brother. Their sister, Susannah, died in 1845. Nearby, I find the graves of their stepbrother, Charles Brown, and step-sister, Mary Isabel Brown, buried in 1848 and 1849, respectively. Franklin scribbles the dates down on the paper with their census information.

Last of all, I discover Davy's grave, flush with the ground and badly eroded. Kneeling in front of it, I brush away dead leaves and dirt to uncover the dates of his life: 1839–1851. Davy was twelve years old when he died.

"Sad," Franklin murmurs. "What do you think happened?"

"Sickness. One after the other." I remember how that felt. First Mother. Then Elliott. And just when we thought our tragedy was over, Father.

"How horrible." Franklin watches me survey the graves and does the thing he has done dozens of times in our long friendship. He reads my mind. "If you don't mind my saying so, Eleanor, I've always thought that losing his wife and son must have driven your father to drink. It was tragic, but you shouldn't hold it against his memory."

If anyone else brought this subject up, I'd be hurt or angry. But I know Franklin's intentions are kind, if misguided. "My father started drinking long before then. It's why my parents were separated and we were living with Grandmother Hall when Mother and Elliott got sick. Father came to see me and Gracie, but only to give us excuses why he couldn't take care of us. And then, the next thing I knew, he was dead too."

It shames me to admit it, but his death haunts me more than my mother's. She died of sickness through no fault of her own, and he died of drink. And yet I loved him. God help me, I loved him.

Suddenly, I straighten and look at Franklin. "Did you see the second wife's grave? Ella Drummond?"

"I didn't," he says. "But I'll look."

We walk up and down the rows of gravestones, pushing aside leaves and shrubbery. We don't find a grave for a woman named Ella or Ellen or any plausible variation with the surname of Drummond.

"What do you think that means?" Franklin asks.

"After losing all her family, maybe she moved away."

"I wouldn't blame her if she did."

Neither would I. In 1840, her home was full to bursting. Eleven years later, she was the only one left.

Franklin suggests we search the other cemetery because, being the last Drummond, perhaps she was mistakenly not buried with her family. Not being in any hurry to return home, I agree. As we walk, we talk about books we have read and Franklin's classes at school. I also tell Franklin about the Vengeful ghost in the house that belonged to my grandparents, what we learned from Aunt Bye, and what we *didn't* learn from her.

"I had no idea," Franklin says. "My father told me that Alice's mother died of a kidney disease, but no one ever mentioned that the family had to flee the house afterward. I think you must be right about your grandfather. It explains why they haven't sold the place. He died how many years before the eruption? Six? That's about right."

It is said that eruptions are most likely to occur between five and fifteen years after death. Davy's eruption, after almost fifty years, is unusual.

"You shouldn't have gone to that house," Franklin says then, frowning. "Promise me you won't do it again, Eleanor. At least, not without me there to look after you."

I have no reason to go back to Number 6 West Fifty-Seventh Street. But his concern warms me from the inside, as if I've drunk a cup of sweet hot tea on a cold day. "I promise."

15

ALICE AND HER AUNT

THE séance gave them the information they were looking for, but Alice notices that no one seems enthusiastic about searching the attic for anything linked to Davy Drummond. She has no desire to go up there alone, and on the day following the séance, her cousins seem to be otherwise engaged.

Helen and Corinne apparently had a spat in the morning, which is strange, because they usually get along despite their three-year age difference. Helen departed in a huff, and Corinne tearfully shut herself away in their shared room. Franklin left the house without mentioning where he was going, and Eleanor hasn't shown her face at all.

Alice blames the ghost for casting a pall over the entire house. What should have been a boisterous ongoing house party among the reunited cousins has become uncomfortable and awkward.

This morning, the ghost emptied the kitchen cabinets and used the contents to create an elaborate pyramid in the center of the room with a box of rat poison balanced on top of it all. Ida cried. Alice spent hours helping her and Maisie put everything back where it belonged.

As for Aunt Bye, the shadows under her eyes suggest another sleepless night. She's worried about Uncle Will, of course, and—based on Alice's memory of Mother Edith's pregnancy complaints—is probably suffering from indigestion and backache. But as much as Alice wants to believe that's all there is to it, she knows in her heart that this haunting is part of the reason her aunt looks so haggard.

Therefore, when an envelope from Uncle Will's solicitor appears in the daily post, Alice hesitates only briefly. It crosses her mind to hide the letter and delay any move from this house—at least until she has rounded up the cousins and pointed them at the attic.

Alice loves this house. But she loves Aunt Bye more.

She finds her aunt in her little sitting room at the back of the house, embroidering a linen cap for the baby. Aunt Bye looks up and smiles when Alice enters, though her face is pale. "Where is everyone? The house is quiet for so many guests."

"Franklin went out, Helen mentioned buying decorations for a party, and I think Corinne is hiding from Maisie's wrath." Alice doesn't bring up the spat between the girls.

"Yes, Helen is planning quite an event, I hear. But before that happens we should gather just the family for a game of charades one evening." Aunt Bye's eyes drop to her work. "I enjoy watching you play."

Alice holds out the solicitor's letter. "This arrived."

Her aunt takes the envelope, glances at the return address, then sets it aside and returns to her embroidery.

"It's from your solicitor," Alice points out.

"Yes."

"About houses you can move into."

"We won't be moving." Her aunt's needle makes quick, neat, stitches.

"But Uncle Will said—"

"Sit beside me for a minute, Alice."

Alice settles onto a footstool in front of her aunt's chair.

Aunt Bye cuts and knots her thread. "When I was a child and very sick, I wasn't supposed to live. And when I did live, I wasn't supposed ever to walk again. Doctors told my parents I'd be slow in the head." She glances at Alice, and the two of them exchange a knowing smile. Doctors. Always underestimating the female gender.

"I had a limp and was deaf in one ear," Aunt Bye goes on, "so no man was ever supposed to love me. Then I met Will. I was supposed to be too old to have a baby, and . . ." She indicates her swollen middle. "Here we are. But this is my only chance. I'll never have another child. This one must be born in this house. He told me so."

"*Who* told you?"

"The ghost did. He whispered it right in here." Aunt Bye taps her deaf ear.

Alice breaks out in goose bumps.

"I know it sounds mad," Aunt Bye admits. "I haven't heard anything in this ear since I was a child, but I hear that ghost every night, whispering to me. If I stay here, I'll be delivered of a healthy son. If I leave, my baby will die."

"But," Alice says plaintively, "it's a *ghost*."

"Yes. Maybe it's a mischief-making ghost that likes to play pranks on the housemaids and worry foolish middle-aged women who ought to know better."

That eases Alice's mind. At least Aunt Bye *knows* how unhinged this sounds.

Aunt Bye leans toward Alice, lowering her voice. "It's also an *unnatural* thing, and who knows that it doesn't have *unnatural* knowledge? Moving house is a great inconvenience, and the ghost may be unsettling, but it's not dangerous. I want to deliver my child in the comfort of my own home."

Alice sits as stiff as a pointer on the scent of game. Aunt Bye doesn't want to leave, and Alice should be relieved. She won't be sent back to Washington.

Nevertheless, it disturbs her that the ghost communicates with her aunt this way. Telling her the baby must be born here. . . . Is it a warning—or a threat?

Down the hall, the front doorbell rings.

Aunt Bye reaches over and grasps Alice's hand. "Please don't tell anyone. I know it sounds ludicrous."

"I promise," Alice says.

Maisie appears in the doorway. "Mrs. Cowles, we have an unexpected situation. You'd better come. You too, Miss Alice."

Alice helps Aunt Bye to stand, waits for the cramp in her aunt's back to subside, and matches her pace to that of an expectant mother. They aren't the first to arrive in the foyer. Corinne gets there first and squeals in delight.

Standing in the foyer beside a suitcase, looking extremely pleased with himself, is Alice's little brother Teddy.

Alice looks from her stunned aunt to her grinning brother and back to her aunt. "This is not my fault," she declares. "I had absolutely nothing to do with this!"

"She's right," says Teddy. "It was entirely my idea."

"You should have been invited in the first place!" Corinne exclaims. "You're almost eleven, after all!"

Aunt Bye is less amused. She orders Maisie to send a telegram to Washington, apprising Teddy's parents of his whereabouts. Then she takes Teddy by the ear and marches him into the parlor.

This cheers Alice greatly. Not only has the haunted pregnant woman transformed back into to her indomitable aunt Bye, but *Alice* is not the one in trouble!

In the parlor, Teddy proudly narrates his story.

"I told the clerk at the train station I was buying a ticket for my grandfather, who suffers from gout and couldn't stand in line. Then I found a family with children and sat close to them on the train. When the conductor came by, I spilled some marbles on the floor, and the other children helped me collect them. The conductor assumed I was part of their family. I got off the train at the Grand Central

Depot and walked here." Teddy sighs wistfully. "It was *too* easy, really. I expected it to be harder."

Aunt Bye puts one hand to her forehead. "What are we going to do with you?"

"Let me join the party, I hope." Teddy looks at them through his spectacles, his eyes bright. "Tell me about the ghost! Can I meet it?"

"Its name is Davy Drummond," Corinne says, "and I'm sure you'll meet it soon enough!"

"Oh, goody!" Teddy exclaims. "Let's go looking for him!"

"No, you will not," Aunt Bye says sharply. "You will go upstairs and put yourself in Franklin's room until decisions are made."

"You're not going to send me back, are you?" Teddy's bright-eyed expression of delight melts into an endearing, heartrending plea. It's a talent that Alice has never mastered.

"To your room." Aunt Bye stares him down, immune to his charm.

Shoulders slumping, Teddy shuffles toward the door. Corinne winks at him as he goes, but Aunt Bye doesn't see it because she turns to Alice and says, "Oh, dear."

"Oh, dear indeed," Alice agrees.

WESTERN UNION
To: 132 EAST 21 ST NEW YORK NY
FEB 18 1898

WIRING MONEY SEND TEDDY HOME NEXT TRAIN
TR

WESTERN UNION
To: 1215 19 ST WASHINGTON DC
FEB 18 1898

CONSIDER LETTING HIM STAY COUSINS ARE HERE
BYE

WESTERN UNION
To: 132 EAST 21 ST NEW YORK NY
FEB 18 1898

EDITH AND I DO NOT WANT HIM REWARDED FOR BAD
BEHAVIOR
TR

WESTERN UNION
To: 1215 19 ST WASHINGTON DC
FEB 18 1898

BE HONEST THEODORE WILL YOU GO TO CUBA
BYE

Western Union

To: 132 EAST 21 ST NEW YORK NY

FEB 18 1898

WAR IS IMMINENT ODDS HIGH I WILL RESIGN POSITION TO
FIGHT IN CUBA IF NEEDED
TR

Western Union

To: 1215 19 ST WASHINGTON DC

FEB 18 1898

ALL THE MORE REASON TEDDY NEEDS COMFORT OF PEERS
EDITH HAS ENOUGH TO HANDLE WITH THE YOUNG ONES
BYE

Western Union

To: 132 EAST 21 ST NEW YORK NY

FEB 18 1898

AS ALWAYS YOUR WISDOM IS A BEACON
UPON REFLECTION TEDDY MAY STAY EDITH AND I SEND
LOVE TO ALL
TR

16

ELEANOR TAKES CHARGE

MIDMORNING, Ida hand delivers a note to me from Aunt Bye's house.

Dear Eleanor,

I hope you and your grandmother are well and sickness has not kept you away. We all would like to see you today. I know I would. We are going to search the attic, and I'm certain you will not want to miss that. We could use your good head!

Your devoted cousin Corinne

I have three choices. I can ignore the note. I can go to Aunt Bye's and tell Corinne and Helen exactly what I heard their friends say about me. Or I can do the easy thing, the quiet thing: go and say nothing. I can be polite and pretend it never happened.

I make the cowardly choice. I can't even claim a moral high ground, because I haven't forgiven or forgotten their words. I just swallow my feelings.

It's like Cooper Bluff every summer. Uncle Theodore lines us up and makes us walk sideways down a hill so steep it's almost a cliff. It terrifies me every single time. Of course *Alice* complains. But in the end, she either comes or gets left behind. That's why I never say a word. I carry my fear like a rock in my stomach all the way down the incline, stumbling and sliding until my feet are firmly on the beach below.

Today, the rock in my stomach will be Corinne's laughter.

Grandmother lets me go with only token grumbles, rather like Alice's complaints on Cooper Bluff. I suspect she wants more details about Teddy's runaway trip from Washington. The news came to us on the servants' grapevine mere minutes after his arrival, and Grandmother will be anxious to pass on the news through her Committee of Correspondence that Edith Roosevelt can't keep track of her children.

At my aunt's house, I pay my respects to Aunt Bye and three lady guests who have brought her gifts of baby gowns and diapers. Aunt Bye introduces me, then rattles off the locations of my cousins. Franklin has gone to an athletic club, while Helen is visiting friends. The rest are in the attic.

"Corinne sent me a note asking me to join them there."

"Yes, they could use your good head," Aunt Bye agrees. Her use of the same phrase Corinne put in her note convinces me that it was written at my aunt's request, and I sink a little deeper inside myself. "Be a dear, won't you, Eleanor? Take this shawl up to my room."

"Of course."

Upstairs in Aunt Bye's room, I fold the shawl and place it on her dresser. Just as I'm turning to leave, a stack of telegrams catches my eye. A word jumps out at me. *War.*

I resist the urge to pry. *It's wrong and a betrayal of my aunt's trust.*

I head toward the door.

Alice would do it.

My feet turn around of their own accord and propel me back to the dresser, where I read the worst news imaginable. War is imminent. Uncle Theodore is planning to resign his job with the Navy Department to fight as a soldier. Thoughts fly at me like hornets from a kicked nest.

Does Alice know?

How can war be imminent when they still don't know the cause of the explosion?

Grandmother said that if war was profitable, it didn't matter what caused the explosion.

Would our government really sacrifice its men in a war for profit?

Thank heavens my brother is a child.

But Franklin is almost old enough to volunteer.

My knees quiver. *Franklin.*

To my shame, my last thought goes to Uncle Will, who is already there on the possible front line of battle, and then to Aunt Bye, on the floor below. Receiving visitors. Accepting gifts. Pretending that she doesn't have a telegram predicting doom on her dresser.

I close my eyes. Uncle Theodore doesn't know everything. He might be wrong.

Leaving Aunt Bye's room the way I found it, I turn toward the servants' stairs and the few extra steps that lead up to the attic floor. The door is thrown open, with light glowing from above. "Halloooo?" I call through the hole.

"Eleanor? Is that you? Thank heavens! We need you!"

When my head rises above the level of the floor and I see what lies ahead of me, I think, *I should escape right now.* Instead, I climb all the way up and gaze at the entirety of the attic, my hands on my hips. Then I glare at Alice.

"Don't look at me like that," she snaps. "You know I'm no good at this."

It's as if every single item in this attic that could contain something else, whether it be trunk, box, or suitcase, has exploded. There's hardly a bare space on the floor to be found, and two of those contain Corinne and Teddy, sitting cross-legged amid the wreckage. "We've been going through everything," Corinne says, "but we don't know what to do with what we find."

Going through everything apparently means lining up dominoes for Teddy and looking at old dress patterns and trying on hats for Corinne. She's wearing a straw atrocity adorned with a stuffed bird and tied under her chin with a ribbon. Half a dozen other hats, equally outrageous, lie in a semi-circle around her.

Alice offers me a package of Pepsin chewing gum, but I wave it away. I tried chewing gum once, and Grandmother said it made me look like a horse munching on hay. "We're supposed to identify things that might be connected to the ghost and dispose of them," I remind them. "Not *play* with them."

Teddy avoids my gaze by cleaning his spectacles. Corinne sheepishly unties the ribbon and removes the bird hat.

"All the toys should go," I say.

"Not the china doll," Corinne counters. "The ghost is a boy."

"Yes, the doll. It could have belonged to one of his sisters."

"You can say that about most things in this attic," Alice says. "Those dress patterns might've belonged to his mother."

"They probably did." I pick one up. "Everyone knows I have *no sense of fashion*, but these dresses look like something from the forties." The words are out of my mouth before I believe I've dared to say them. It's something Alice would do: throw the words of someone's unkind conversation back at them. But Corinne shows no recognition. She nods her understanding and starts gathering the patterns into stacks.

"What about the big things?" Teddy asks. "Like the curio cabinet and the linen press?"

"We'll get help for those." I pick my way around the clothing and boxes strewn across the floor, looking at what we must deal with. "What's under here?" I pick up the edge of a blanket that's been thrown over a piece of furniture.

"A rocking chair." Alice speaks in a steady voice, but there's something about her tone that makes me look at her. "The last time I was up here, the ghost sat in that chair, rocking it."

"But it's got a broken runner."

"Yes," says Alice.

"It *definitely* has to go." I drop the edge of the blanket with a shiver. "Teddy, I want you to get paper and pen and list the big things—the furniture, the rugs, the draperies—with as much description as you can. We'll show the list to Aunt Bye and see if she can't recall some of the items. If she knows the rugs, for instance, used to be hers, then we don't have to bother with them."

Teddy nods and scrambles down the stairs to fetch a pen and paper.

"The rest of us will make piles. Things that definitely need to be discarded and things that can stay. See if there are any we can eliminate."

Alice points across the room. "There's a box of letters that belong to the Morrows, and the dates on those magazines are from only twenty years ago."

"Good. They can stay."

Corinne's cheeks dimple. "See? I told you we needed Eleanor."

Alice kicks a cardboard box. "This should be burned. It looks like everything in here belonged to the Drummonds."

"Burned?" The box is filled to the brim with yellowed papers. The ones on top are typewritten and look like legal documents. "Shouldn't we read them first?"

"You can if you want." Alice shrugs. "I'm not going to."

It feels wrong to burn important-looking contracts without at least glancing through them. But we need to remove all the belongings of the Drummonds from this house. I test the weight of the box, finding it quite heavy. "We'll ask Franklin to carry it down from the attic and bring it to my house. I'll look through the box and burn the papers when I'm finished."

Teddy returns and begins to make his list. Corinne puts the toys back in their metal box. Alice and I pick up the scattered clothes, shoes, and hats and shove them into trunks and suitcases, pushing those closer to the stairs in what becomes our "discard" area. We work for an hour or more. Slowly the disaster I walked into begins to look more manageable.

Alice is quiet, and I wonder if she knows about the telegram on Aunt Bye's dresser. When Corinne and Teddy start dragging suitcases down the stairs, she says in a voice meant for my hearing alone, "Eleanor, I need to tell you something. Aunt Bye asked me not to, but I think I must."

I brace myself, confident that, for once, I know the bad news before it's delivered. But instead of telling me that her father is going to war, Alice informs me that the ghost has been whispering in Aunt Bye's deaf ear that her baby will die unless he's born in this house. My mouth falls open. "Do you think . . ." I don't know how to ask Alice if our aunt is losing her mind.

"I believe her," Alice says. "Because the ghost spoke to me too. Days ago. I thought it was my imagination at the time, but now I know."

"What did it say?"

Alice looks away. "It was something cruel, and I don't want to repeat it."

"You don't have to," I assure her. Things said to a person in cruelty are very personal.

Then I gasp.

"What?" Alice demands.

Pressing both hands to my cheeks, I turn around so that I can have a moment of privacy. Alice waits more patiently than I expect her to, but when I face her again, her eyes are direct and piercing. "Two days ago, I was standing at the back kitchen door, and I overheard a conversation between Helen's friends in the front parlor."

"You can't hear people talking in the parlor from the back kitchen door."

"Exactly."

Alice's eyes narrow. "I'm guessing what you overheard wasn't to your liking, because you left that day without telling anyone and didn't come back yesterday either."

I nod.

Alice plops to a seat on top of one of the trunks. "This is a strange ghost."

I agree. Glancing around the attic, I wonder if it's

watching us now. The air is cold, but not unnaturally so. I can't see our breath in the air. But does that mean anything?

"I have an idea," Alice announces. "The day after the eruption, a woman from the Supernatural Registry board came to the house to collect information. She said that if we found out anything else about this ghost, we should inform her, for their records. We could visit her, tell her what we know and what's going on. Maybe she can help."

"That's a very good idea."

Alice smiles broadly. "Eleanor, *wait* until I tell you the woman's name!"

"Why? Do you think I know her?"

17

ALICE CHALLENGES AN EXPERT

UNT Bye agrees that the woman from the Supernatural Registry board asked to be informed if they identified the progenitor of their ghost. "But Alice, I think she meant for you to send a letter. Not pester her at her office."

Then Aunt Bye looks at Eleanor—who is practically bouncing in her seat—and revelation dawns. "Oh. You want to *meet* her, don't you?"

Ever since finding out that the woman from the Supernatural Registry board is in fact Nellie Bly, female journalist extraordinaire, Eleanor has been grinning from ear to ear. She isn't even doing that silly thing where she hides her teeth behind her hand.

Eleanor's beaming face wins over Aunt Bye. She gives them permission and asks Maisie to hire a cab with instructions to convey them downtown and wait for their return trip. Pressing a few bills for the fare into Alice's hand, Aunt Bye says, "Don't take up too much of her time, and don't be disappointed if she's too busy to see you."

When the cab approaches downtown Manhattan, Alice's eyes fix on the *New York World* Building, the tallest skyscraper in New York City and the place Nellie Bly once worked as a reporter. But, disappointingly, the cab stops in front of a two-story building made of dingy gray stone, adorned with a corroded iron plaque that reads: EW YORK CITY S PERN TURAL REG STRY.

Inside, the girls find themselves in a long corridor with an open room at the end. Eleanor hesitates, reverting to shyness, but Alice strides forward, her shoes clacking on the floor.

Inside the large room, eight women sit at desks. Their heads are bent to their tasks, typing information onto forms that are then stacked into baskets. Two more women circle the room, collecting papers from the baskets and filing them in cabinets. All are dressed miserably alike in white or beige shirtwaists with no adornment and dark skirts. There isn't a hint of color in the room.

The lady at the closest desk looks up. "Can I help you?"

"Alice and Eleanor Roosevelt to see Nellie Bly."

The woman creases her brow and purses her lips.

"Mrs. Seaman," Alice corrects herself.

"May I inquire what your business is with Mrs. Seaman?"

"She visited my home after an eruption and asked me

to inform her of any additional information we discovered."

The woman smiles in an indulgent manner. "You may leave your information with me and rest assured that it will be properly entered into the record."

"But we wanted to see her."

"We have questions!" Eleanor suddenly finds her voice. "Our aunt is expecting a baby, and this ghost has not been good for her health!"

"Girls—" the woman begins.

Another, stronger voice intervenes. "Joan! Let them in."

Alice snaps her head around to see Mrs. Seaman standing in a doorway, her arms crossed and one shoulder leaning against the doorframe. Her bright yellow dress brightens the drab room the way the sun banishes a cloudy day. Her eyes are alight with amusement, and her demeanor is that of a cocksure reporter. Whatever she chooses to call herself, this woman will always be the one and only Nellie Bly.

Joan sighs and waves them in. Knowing Eleanor as she does, Alice grabs her by the hand to prevent her from wavering under Sour Joan's disapproval.

"Miss Roosevelt," Miss Bly addresses Alice in greeting, then looks at her companion.

"May I present my cousin Eleanor Roosevelt?"

Eleanor, poor awkward thing, sticks one foot behind the other and curtsies, like she's being introduced to royalty. Miss Bly laughs, although not in an unkind way, and beckons them into her office.

The room contains a desk with two wooden chairs

in front for visitors and a cushioned chair behind it for Miss Bly.

"How can I help you, girls?" Miss Bly asks. "I heard you tell Joan that you're worried for your aunt."

Alice glances at Eleanor and, seeing that her cousin is still struck mute, takes command of the conversation. She names the ghost's progenitor, along with the date of his death and his age. Miss Bly takes notes. "What manifestations have you experienced?"

Alice starts with the benign ones, like the handkerchief, and Eleanor volunteers that the ghost made her tea. Then come the less charming phenomena: the snake, the rat, the stacked chairs, and the ransacked kitchen. Finally, Alice describes the events that disturb her: the doom-threatening whispers in her aunt's deaf ear and Eleanor's overhearing a distressing conversation at an improbable distance.

Nellie Bly listens intently. "You have a very interesting ghost," she says when Alice finishes. "First, there's an unusually long dormancy between the progenitor's death and the eruption of the ghost. Forty-seven years."

"Is that significant?"

"Experts disagree. There's evidence to suggest that secret deaths result in longer dormancies, but Davy Drummond was buried in a cemetery, not under the floorboards, so that doesn't seem to be the case here. Deaths that involve intense or drawn-out emotional trauma are also thought to cause lengthy dormancies—or sometimes extremely short ones." Miss Bly turns her hands up in a gesture of surrender.

"However, the majority of deaths result in no ghost at all, so there are some experts who claim it's entirely random."

Eleanor sits up at the mention of *drawn-out emotional trauma*. Alice nudges her cousin's elbow. "You've thought of something. What is it?"

Eleanor's cheeks flush when Miss Bly's gaze turns toward her, but she states her case. "When Davy was a baby, ten people lived in his house. He had parents, brothers and sisters, and a nephew the same age he was. Eleven years later, they were all dead except for his mother. They died one by one, sometimes two in the same year."

"You're thinking there was chronic illness in the family?" Miss Bly asks. "Something contagious that killed them slowly, like consumption?"

Eleanor nods. "It happened to my family, to a smaller degree."

"I'm sorry to hear that," Miss Bly says gravely. "There is no smaller degree when it comes to bereavement. I'm sure it affected you greatly."

"But Miss Bly!" Alice bursts out. "Is this really a Friendly ghost? After all the horrid things it's done?"

"What other kind can it be? It's not an Unaware. It responds to the living. It's not a Vengeful. It hasn't harmed you." Alice starts to object, but Miss Bly preempts her. "While it has played pranks and hurt your feelings, it hasn't tried to *kill* you. Nevertheless, the auditory manifestations are unusual. Ghosts sometimes speak, though typically they only repeat things they said in life. They don't make hurtful comments directed at specific individuals. Has anyone else in the house experienced this? Your uncle, perhaps?"

Eleanor shakes her head. "Uncle Will was sent to Cuba."

But the question makes Alice wonder. She and Aunt Bye aren't the only people living in the house. What about the cousins, the maids? Has the ghost been whispering to them as well? She recalls yesterday's spat between Corinne and Helen and how easily Ida burst into tears over one of Davy's pranks.

"Your haunting may be out of the ordinary," Miss Bly continues, "but I don't think you have reason to be alarmed. The designation Friendly only means that these ghosts thrive on interaction with the living, not that they are pleasant company." She sighs. "In any case, the ghost is aware of the living activities in the house, and it hasn't tried to physically harm you. By process of elimination, it must be a Friendly."

Alice wants to argue the point but knows that if she states her idea outright, it will be rejected. She struggles for a few seconds, then offers up something intensely personal— even though she knows how it will sound to Eleanor, and that it will probably make Nellie Bly regard her with pity.

"My stepmother says there are two types of girls. Obedient girls like Eleanor, who are loved by everyone. And contrary girls, who will never be respected or loved." Alice pretends she doesn't hear the little gasp from Eleanor. Instead she lifts her chin and addresses Nellie Bly. "I don't intend to fall into either category."

"Good for you," Miss Bly responds without an ounce

of pity in her voice. "You're a girl after my own heart. But you see the difference, don't you? The ghost categories were established by experts in the field, not a woman trying to coerce her stepdaughter into obedience."

"But . . ." Alice plunges on. "Experts said you couldn't pose as a patient in an asylum for a week and come out with a story. But you did. Experts said you couldn't travel all the way around the world in eighty days like Jules Verne's Phileas Fogg. But you did—in seventy-two days."

Eleanor pipes up unexpectedly, scooting forward in her chair. "Experts in the Middle Ages said ghosts were summoned by witches, and experts in the last century believed all ghosts must be murder victims. Now experts say there are three categories, but how do we know they're any more correct than the experts who were disproved? Maybe, fifty years from now, *our* experts will be called crackpots."

Miss Bly rises and paces behind her desk, fingers pressed to her lips. The cousins exchange nervous glances. Just when Alice thinks they are seconds from being thrown out of the office—and Eleanor looks downright terrified that she has offended her idol—a smile bows Nelly's lips. She faces her visitors again, placing both hands on her desk and leaning forward.

"Girls, I need to consult someone. An expert in his own way, although many people term him"—she winks at Eleanor—"a crackpot. It's difficult to capture his attention when he's obsessed with one of his own projects. But I believe he'll have an interest in your ghost."

Opening a cupboard, Nelly dons a coat—a scarlet bolero with stitched black borders—and snatches up a matching hat with black swan feathers that makes Alice green with envy.

Instead of dismissing her guests, Nellie Bly vanishes through the door, leaving Alice and Eleanor to find their own way out.

18

ELEANOR DISCOVERS THE VALUE OF A LIFE

I met Nellie Bly! I almost dance past stern Joan, down the dingy hall, and onto the street. *She listened to me. I gave her an idea that made her run out of her office!*

My high spirits are squelched within seconds of boarding the cab that is waiting for us when I ask Alice, "What shall we tell everyone?"

"Nothing."

"Nothing? What do you mean, *nothing*?"

Alice squirms in her seat. "She said there was no danger, remember? We'll wait until she consults her expert or crackpot or whatever he is, and *then* decide what to do."

"But we just convinced her that the ghost might not be a Friendly. That there may have been a misdiagnosis. And you want to tell Aunt Bye *nothing*?"

"There's nothing to tell her—only that the Supernatural

Registry wants to look into our haunting a little more—and if we say even that" —Alice's eyes meet mine, and to my surprise, they are pleading—"she'll know I broke my promise to her."

"But . . ." I bite off my objection. Alice broke her promise for the best reasons possible. However, like a shattered teacup, once a trust is broken, it *might* be glued together, but it will probably never again hold tea.

"All right," I agree reluctantly. "As long as you watch over her and—"

"Of course I will!" Alice snaps.

Our conversation ends there. That night, after I take a cold supper with Grandmother and regale her with my story of meeting the famous Nellie Bly (*"You mean that upstart woman from Pittsburgh who thought her travels were newsworthy?"*), I worry that making that promise to Alice was a mistake. Miss Bly admitted our haunting was unusual. What if something terrible happens because we didn't warn everyone?

When there's a knock on the kitchen door the next day, I rush past Rosie to open it in case it's bad news from Aunt Bye's house.

Franklin stands outside in his shirtsleeves, snow dusting his hat and something bulky in his arms. I open the door wider to let him in, and Rosie exclaims, "Goodness, Master Franklin! What are you doing out there with no coat on?"

Franklin stomps snow off his shoes and steps inside. "It started snowing when I was halfway here, and I didn't want the papers to get wet." He sets his burden on the floor and whips off what I now realize is his coat. Underneath is the cardboard box of documents from Aunt Bye's attic. "I brought it around back because I didn't think your grand-mother would want this coming through her house."

I see his point. I didn't notice when it was in the attic because everything there is so grimy, but the box is streaked with cobwebs and dust. Grandmother will have a con-niption if she sees it. Rosie isn't keen on it either. "What is this?" she asks with distaste.

"Documents I need to sort through and then burn," I tell her.

"You should burn them *first*," she mutters.

Franklin shrugs his coat on, preparing to leave imme-diately. "You must be freezing," I protest. "Stay for a cup of tea. Or coffee." Franklin is fond of coffee, a taste he picked up from Uncle Theodore, who drinks nearly a gallon of the bitter brew a day.

"Can't." He turns up his collar. "I have my marching orders. We're emptying the attic today."

"Emptying it completely?"

"Almost. The street cleaners won't be very happy with us. Oh!" He snaps his fingers and points at me. "I almost for-got. You're invited for charades tonight. Helen insists."

I glance out the kitchen window. "I'll come if the snow stops."

"If the snow doesn't stop, we'll send a cab," Franklin says. "Pack a bag and stay overnight in Alice's room. It's hardly a real reunion when one of us isn't there."

I feel my cheeks grow warm and pretend to be interested in the box of documents. I thank Franklin for bringing it. He tips his hat, grins, and steps out into the snow.

As soon as he's gone, I sit down at the kitchen table and apply myself to the unpleasant task of sorting through the filthy box. The first few documents are papers concerned with the purchase of the house. Next is a life insurance policy for Edgar Drummond and several bills of sale. It turns out we were right. The dress patterns belonged to Davy's mother, and so did the dressmaker's dummy. Mrs. Drummond was a seamstress.

None of the papers pertain to Davy's haunting, however, and my mind wanders while I stack them in a discard pile. I think about what I need to pack for a night at Aunt Bye's and whether emptying the attic will really diminish the ghost's power to torment the living residents. Several more papers go into the discard pile with barely a glance.

Then I'm holding Susannah Drummond's life insurance policy in my hand, staring at it with an unsettling feeling that I might be overlooking something important. "Rosie, how does life insurance work?"

Rosie, chopping carrots, glances over her shoulder at me. "You purchase a policy and pay a small fee every year to maintain it. If the person covered by the insurance dies, the beneficiary of the policy receives a sum of money the company has agreed upon."

"Is it usual to buy a policy for a young person? Or a child?"

This time Rosie pauses, and her answer is more hesitant. "Life insurance policies are usually purchased for adults. But . . . if an older child has a job that helps provide for the family, I *suppose* one might purchase insurance to protect that income. As for a young child . . . I don't believe an insurance company would pay out very much—maybe enough to cover the cost of a decent burial."

A *decent* burial. The image of Davy's flat stone flashes through my mind, the letters so shallowly carved they had almost worn away.

I examine the paper in my hand. Susannah Drummond, age sixteen, was insured in 1844 for one hundred dollars in the event of her death. The beneficiary of the policy was her stepmother, Ella Drummond.

I dig through the discard pile, pulling out the policy for Edgar Senior and two more that I shifted without paying attention: policies for Edgar Junior and Benjamin, the Drummond brothers who died in the same year. Both of them were insured in 1843, the sum of their lost wages listed as compensation to the beneficiary of the policy.

Who happened to be their stepmother, Ella Drummond.

I paw through the box, tossing aside Ella's bills of sale for her dressmaking and other unrelated documents and singling out the insurance policies. Because there are more.

Ella's husband and stepsons were insured through one insurance company, but she switched to a different one for her stepdaughter, Susannah. For her son, Charles, and her daughter, Mary Isabel, she signed with a third company.

I don't have their death dates in front of me because Franklin recorded them at the cemetery and took the notes back to Aunt Bye's house. Nevertheless, I have a general idea of the order in which these people died, and it seems as if Ella took out a life insurance policy on each of them a year or so before they passed.

If Rosie is right, it is reasonable to take out insurance on the people who contribute income to your home. But it's beyond reason to predict the order in which they will die. That's what stands out to me as I lay the policies on the kitchen table and examine the dates they were signed. I'm certain that the order in which these young people were insured by Ella Drummond is the same order in which they died.

Rummaging through the box, I pull out more bills of sale until finally, in the bottom of the box, I locate the document I'm looking for, one last policy. The insured: David Drummond, age eleven. The beneficiary: Ella Drummond, age forty-two.

The value of the policy . . . My hand trembles.

Thirty dollars.

The value of Davy Drummond's life was thirty dollars.

I drop the document and stand up so quickly, I nearly overturn my chair.

"Miss Eleanor!" Rosie turns to face me. "What's wrong?"

"Rosie—" I can hardly bring myself to say it. "I think she killed them. The mother. She insured them, killed them, and collected the money."

"No! That's impossible! No woman would do that. Not to her own children!" Rosie puts a hand to her heart, no doubt thinking of her little grandchildren.

But Mrs. Drummond didn't start with her own children. She started with her husband, moved on to her stepchildren, and when she ran out of those . . . *then* came her own flesh and blood.

"She wouldn't have gotten away with it," Rosie insists. "Someone would've noticed. The authorities . . . a doctor . . . someone . . ."

But evidence seems to show she *did* get away with it.

People get sick or injured every day, and sometimes they die. I lost three-fourths of my family in the span of two years. Alice's mother and grandmother died within days of each other. The Drummond family deaths were spaced out over a decade. Maybe no one suspected.

I look at Rosie. "I have to show these to Aunt Bye."

Her eyes dart between the papers and my face. She has stopped trying to tell me I'm wrong. "Yes, maybe you should." She opens a cupboard and pulls out the leather satchel she uses for shopping when the weather is bad. "I'll put them in here so they don't get wet."

While Rosie packs the papers into the satchel, I fetch my coat and hat. Aunt Bye will *have* to move out of that house when she sees these insurance policies. Regardless of what that ghost whispers in her deaf ear, she won't want to live in a house where all those people were . . . what? Poisoned? Smothered? Pushed down the stairs?

Did Davy know? Did he know how his brothers and sisters died, one by one, and why? When he was the last one left with his mother, did he know he was next? Did he wake up every morning and go to sleep every night wondering when his mother would decide she'd like to have thirty dollars?

I can't bear the thought.

✣ 19 ✣

ALICE GOES HOME

WHEN Alice catches Teddy and Corinne whispering in the hallway on the second floor, she chastises them for dawdling. "Let's go!" She claps her hands noisily. "Those musty old carpets aren't going to roll downstairs by themselves!"

Teddy pushes his glasses up his nose with his index finger and growls, "All right, Sissy. We'll be right there. You don't need to order us around."

His tone of voice startles her. It isn't like her brother to be short-tempered.

"I do if you're standing idle," Alice mutters, stomping up to the attic. *She* hasn't stopped moving since the purge began, and now that it's snowing, she's even more anxious to get the attic cleared before her cousins revolt and call it half a day on account of the weather.

They *must* clear the attic of everything that could

possibly hold Davy Drummond here. Alice is hopeful their efforts are already having an effect, because there haven't been any ghostly manifestations, friendly or otherwise, all day.

She makes two more trips up and down the stairs, lugging boxes and smaller, manageable items of furniture, before noticing that she hasn't seen Teddy or Corinne since she spoke to them in the hallway.

Alice checks the kitchen, but Maisie hasn't seen them. They aren't in the billiards room or the parlor or Aunt Bye's sitting room. Finally, she asks Helen, who has chosen for herself the arduous task of opening and closing the front door to the people doing the actual carrying. "They left on an errand," Helen says, "half an hour ago or more."

"What errand?"

"I don't know. I assumed *you* sent them." Helen peers through the sidelight window and opens the front door for Franklin.

"Where have *you* been?" Alice demands.

Franklin shakes snow off his coat. "You told me to deliver that box to Eleanor. Remember?"

What Alice remembers is asking *Teddy* to take the box to Eleanor—and Franklin jumping in to volunteer. Normally, she'd pursue that topic until Franklin blushed, but right now she has other fish to fry. "Teddy and Corinne have gone off somewhere. Do you have any idea where?"

She expects him to say no, so when the color drains from his face, her heart pounds. "He left?" Franklin says. "They both left?"

"You know where they went!" Alice exclaims. "Tell me!"

Franklin spreads his hands. "I don't know for sure . . . but he heard me talking to you this morning, Helen." Helen puts a hand over her mouth, and her eyes go wide.

"Where did he go?"

"I'm sorry, Alice. Eleanor told me about your grand-mother's house—and your grandfather's ghost. Yesterday, the athletic club I visited was so close to that street, I stopped by. Just to see the outside. I told Helen about it."

Alice's heart drops straight to her stomach. "Teddy heard you talking."

Franklin nods. "I told him I'd seen the house. But he acted as if he already knew about the haunting. You don't think . . ."

Teddy didn't know. No more than Alice knew. But he would lie, to save face.

He has run off to see the house that his half sister was born in, that his grandmother died in, and that his grand-father haunts as a Vengeful. Didn't Alice do the same thing when Eleanor told *her*? And of course Corinne went with him. Whenever one of those two wanders into trouble, the other always provides faithful companionship.

Franklin runs a hand through his hair. "What are we going to do?"

"We'll go after them," says Helen.

"They'll be fine. *I* looked at the house and came to no harm," Franklin states in a voice meant to be reassuring. "So did Alice and Eleanor."

That is true, but Alice remembers what she heard . . .

Alice. Come home.

What if that scritch-scratch voice calls to Teddy?

"I'm sure they'll be fine." But Helen grimly follows that up with, "We'll go with protection."

"Iron?" Franklin asks.

"And salt."

While Franklin and Helen dash off to grab what they need, Alice doesn't dare wait another second. Teddy and Corinne have been gone more than half an hour and must be halfway there by now. Pausing only to grab the first coat that comes to hand, she rushes out the front door and immediately collides with someone walking up the steps.

"Alice?" It's Eleanor, carrying a satchel.

"Teddy's in danger!" Alice pushes Eleanor toward the door. "They'll explain. I'm going ahead. Tell them to hurry!"

Slipping and sliding on the sidewalk, Alice soon regrets the lack of a hat and wonders if she should have waited for her cousins after all. The snow falls faster and heavier. Her ears sting, and her wet hair drips inside the collar of the too-large coat she borrowed. Ducking her head, she concentrates on keeping her footing and not pitching face-first into the street.

"Hello there, miss!"

Shielding her eyes from the falling snow, Alice looks up to see a covered grocery wagon stopping beside her in the street. Gazing at her with worry from the driver's seat is a kindly faced grocer. A pigtailed girl of about ten years sits beside him.

"Do you need help, child?" the grocer asks. "A ride, perhaps?"

"Yes." Lies spill out of Alice's mouth as fast as she can think them up. "My aunt has taken ill, and I must tell my father to come at once. He lives—" Remembering her current state of dress and the grandeur of the houses at her destination, she amends her words. "He *works* at Number Six West Fifty-Seventh Street. No, I'm sorry. I mean Number *Sixteen*." Number 6 is conspicuously labeled as Unsafe; her lie will come apart at the seams if the grocer delivers her there. Better to run the last block than be delayed with nosy questions from a well-meaning adult.

"Help her up, Pearl," the man says, and the girl holds out a hand.

Alice takes it, her hand a block of ice in the warmth of the girl's mittened one. Pearl scoots closer to her father on the bench to make room. "Thank you!" Alice gasps.

Pearl examines Alice with worried eyes. "You're frozen almost to death, aren't you?"

"Lucky we've finished our deliveries and it's not out of our way," her father says.

"Pa, you'd take her even if we had deliveries and it was a mile out of our way."

This is a lucky break. Teddy and Corinne must be slowed by the snow. Alice might even get there before them. Still, she jiggles up and down on the bench, wishing the horse would go faster. Traffic gets heavier the farther downtown they go. People have business despite the weather, and the poor visibility and everyone's desire for right-of-way at every intersection slow them down. Luckily, the grocer and his daughter don't pester her with questions. Pearl finds a rag for Alice to dry her face, and Alice tries not to mind that it smells of onions.

Finally, they reach Fifty-Seventh Street, and Alice launches herself out of the wagon when the grocer slows the horse at an intersection. "This is close enough! Thank you!"

"You get yourself warmed up, you hear!" Pearl calls.

Alice waves an arm in the air and hopes they take that as thanks and dismissal. Her head swivels back and forth as she looks for Teddy and Corinne. As before, the block is deserted. Having started from the wagon at a dead run, Alice forces her legs to slow as she approaches Number 6. The snow on the sidewalk makes an unbroken carpet ahead of her. Her footprints alone disturb the snowfall.

She heaves a sigh. She has beaten them. All she has to do is wait in front of Number 6 for the rest of the cousins to arrive. If Teddy and Corinne appear, she'll deal with them, although it is possible that the snow made them turn around and go home. The panic she felt when she learned her brother was coming here subsides . . .

And then spikes, shooting her heart rate up so fast her throat throbs.

Two sets of footprints cross the street at an angle, heading for Number 6. They come up onto the sidewalk and merge into an area of churned-up snow that stretches the entire length of the old Roosevelt residence.

"Teddy!" Alice yells. "Corinne!"

She traverses the length of the house, past the windows through which, on her previous visit, she glimpsed furniture, to the screened-in porch. Here, to her horror, she sees indentations in the snow on the *other* side of the decorative iron fence leading right up to the porch—and from there to a screen door hanging loose on its hinges.

"No, no, no!" How could they be so foolish? "Teddy! Corinne!" Alice climbs the fence, straddles it in her divided skirt, and jumps down on the other side. Immediately the damp cold of a February day shifts to something sharper and biting. Alice's wet hair freezes in place. Every snowflake that lands on her face burns. Instinct wails at her to flee, but her legs drive her forward, one step at a time. "Teddy!"

Teddy. Her baby brother. Not her new baby brother, but the *original*. The one she hugged like a doll when she was hardly more than a toddler herself and—to the aggravation of Mother Edith—defended against all visitors. "Don't touch!" she had yelled at a vicar's wife. "Ted-deeee!" she calls into the house now.

Her answer is a scream—high-pitched, thrumming with terror. Corinne.

Alice slaps the broken screen door open and plunges onto the porch. Darkness drops over her, despite the lack of solid walls. There is an *outside* to the house and an *inside*. The porch is *inside*, by the rules of this haunting. Inside is cold, like shards of glass, and dark, like the gullet of a predator.

Double glass doors connecting the porch to the house

swing open, leading Alice into the huge drawing room she glimpsed through the windows on her last visit. She sees the grandfather clock, sofas, tall vases, and a piano. There are elk and bear heads mounted on the walls, much as in her father's current home. On a low table, Alice spots a half-completed baby blanket in an embroidery hoop, the needle still piercing the fabric as if the embroiderer laid it aside mere minutes ago. Its once-bright colors are muted with dust. Alice is drawn to it. It might have been her mother who set this down, meaning to finish it on a day that never came. Alice is reaching for it when her mind is jolted by a shout from upstairs—Teddy's voice—and another harrowing scream from Corinne.

Alice shakes her head to clear the fuzziness. *What am I doing?* Abandoning the baby blanket, Alice forces herself onward. *Teddy's in danger! Corinne needs my help!* But every step is a struggle. The room's proportions aren't right; shadows move where they shouldn't.

The room ends with a door that opens to a high-ceilinged foyer. Similar to the entranceway in Miss Barnstable's house next door, there are twin marble staircases that curve up to the second floor. Blinking fiercely to stay focused, Alice climbs the steps. "Teddy!"

"Alice!" Corinne shrieks. "Alice, help us!"

On the second floor, nothing looks right. A corridor telescopes in front of her, stretching the same way Aunt Bye's front hall did on the day after the eruption. Alice fumbles through the first open doorway . . .

. . . and finds Corinne cowering on the floor, the bow

torn from her hair and red marks around her throat. Teddy stands in front of her. His glasses are broken, hanging crookedly from one ear, and his hands are braced on the top rail of a crib, which he holds as a barrier in front of himself and Corinne. *My crib. That is my crib.*

Then Alice's attention shifts to the figure on the other side of the room.

It's a full-body physical manifestation, like Eleanor's uncle Valentine. But while Valentine Hall is faded almost to transparency, this ghost is visible in its entirety, every fold of its white dressing gown crisp and clean as if the cotton garment were newly purchased and pressed.

"Get away from them!" Alice screams.

The vision turns like the hand of a clock jerking from minute to minute.

Every feature of the apparition is familiar to Alice—the heart-shaped face, the little bow mouth, the direct gaze of the eyes.

It's the same face that peers out of the photograph beside her bed. Her mother, Alice Hathaway Lee Roosevelt.

DEATHS ATTRIBUTED TO VENGEFULS
IN U.S., BY CAUSE, 1897

Asphyxiation (Gas)	1,312
Blunt Trauma	77
Drowning	9
Fall	56
Fire	1,566
Heart Failure	40
Hypothermia	2,015
Poisoning	112
Stabbing	3
Strangulation	127
Suffocation	339

20

ELEANOR REMEMBERS "WE'RE ROOSEVELTS"

HIRING a cab in a snowstorm is almost impossible to start with, and when the fare is three young people slinging iron fire implements over their shoulders and carrying a bag of salt, one might as well hope for a passing unicorn. After the third cab refuses to stop for us, we resign ourselves to walking.

I clench my fireplace shovel in both hands and crane my neck, searching the street. "Do you see Alice? I was hoping we could catch up with her."

Franklin shakes his head. "She could've cut across Madison Square Park or caught a cab."

A cab? That seems unlikely, but if anyone could find a unicorn, it would be Alice.

"Is this Twenty-Fourth Street?" Helen stops suddenly and peers at a street sign. "I know what to do. You two—stay here."

"Stay here?" I exclaim. "Alice asked us to hurry."

"*Stay here,*" Helen repeats. "Trust me." Tucking the salt under one arm and picking up her skirts, she breaks into a very un-Helenish canter across the street and around the corner.

I pace. What in the world possessed Alice to go after Teddy and Corinne without waiting for us? As the snow falls more heavily, gray clouds press down, squeezing the heavens closer to the street. I turn to Franklin. "I have to go. I can't let her down."

He nods, hefting a poker over his shoulder and taking my arm. "We'll go together."

Before we've taken more than a few steps, the blast of a horn slices through the snow-muffled street. From the corner where we last saw Helen, a large carriage appears, oddly shaped and lacking a horse. Instead of the *clip-clop* of hooves, its approach is heralded by a horrible grinding noise and a dark cloud.

I recognize this motorcar. There are only two or three in the whole city, and this one frequently passes by Grandmother's house, making its terrible racket and belching smoke. Usually it's driven by a large, bearded man, but today a boy in his teens holds the tiller. He's bundled up in a coat, scarf, hat, and goggles. Helen sits beside him, waving at us.

"It's George with his father's Benz!" Franklin exclaims. I assume this must be the George who called upon Helen on her first day in town and stayed for the séance.

The vehicle huffs and puffs to a stop in front of us. "I

hear you need transport!" George shouts over the motor of what Grandmother calls *that infernal contraption.*

"Does it go faster than we can walk?" Franklin asks doubtfully.

"It goes twenty miles an hour!" George crows.

We climb aboard. "Good thinking, Helen!" Franklin says.

"Good thing George talks constantly about this motorcar," Helen replies. "Or I'd never have remembered it was nearby."

The Benz has an overhead cover but no windows to protect us from the snow and wind that pick up when the vehicle accelerates. The sting is so painful that we pull our hats and bonnets down as low as they will go and shelter against one another.

The motorcar slides precariously through every intersection, its brakes no match for the slippery roads. Luckily, the horse-drawn carriages give us a wide berth. Between our speed, our lack of ability to stop, and the wariness of the general public, we arrive at the old Roosevelt house in a matter of minutes. George pulls off his goggles and gapes at the abandoned mansion with the yellow UNSAFE sign. "You aren't going in there, are you?"

"We will if we have to," Helen replies grimly.

Franklin runs to the fence that borders the house and peers at the snow on the other side. He shouts something I don't catch and points at the house, specifically at the screened-in porch. My heart sinks as I sense evil watching us through the window eyes of the mansion. It lured in

Teddy and Corinne, against common sense, and possibly Alice too. Now it's beckoning to us.

Franklin clambers over the fence. Helen runs to catch up with him—leaving George sputtering and protesting behind her—and I pelt after her through the snow. If we're going to enter that deathtrap, we should go in together, not in dribs and drabs, the easier to be made victims.

"Maybe you girls should stay with George," Franklin says worriedly, turning back to meet us when we start climbing the fence.

"Make yourself useful, Uncle Franklin," Helen replies, "and take this." She hands him the sack of salt and hauls her skirt over the top of the enclosure. I throw my fireplace shovel over first, then clamber up. My unfashionably short skirt and thick stockings make for better climbing attire than Helen's Gibson Girl dress. It takes both me and Franklin to untangle her. At last we gather up our weapons and stumble into the cursed house while thunder rumbles through the weighted clouds.

"We should stay together," Franklin whispers, echoing my own thoughts. I tighten my grip on the shovel, not sure what I'm supposed to do with it but willing to do what I can.

Inside the house, the cold bites and claws at us like a ferocious animal. Outside, thunder rumbles again. As the rumble trails off, the tail end of a scream filters down from the second floor.

I run. Or rather, my brain tells my body to run, but

the haunting's grip on me is so tight that nothing happens. The others don't run either, despite the fact that one of our beloved cousins just cried out in terror. The air crackles as, bunched together, we cross a drawing room and reach the front of the house. Forcing my legs to mount each step of the marble staircase, I feel like an ant slogging through marmalade. My fingers cling to the back of Franklin's coat even though they're senseless with cold.

A shout. A crash. Another scream.

On the second floor, Franklin looks into a room, and I let go of his coat as he barrels over the threshold. Helen drops the bag of salt in the doorway before following him in. Clinging to the doorjamb, I stare at the nightmare inside.

Corinne huddles in a corner, her face streaked with tears. Teddy struggles to climb out from beneath an infant's crib, which has overturned on him. That was the crash. And Alice . . . Alice is pressed against a wall, thrashing and struggling for breath while a ghost tries to strangle the life out of her. The shock of what I'm seeing nearly sends me to my knees.

It's Alice's mother. Dear heaven, help us. It's Alice's mother.

I recognize it from the photograph Alice keeps on her bedside table, and even if I didn't, I'd know it by the eyes. They're the same color and shape as Alice's, except that right now, Alice's eyes are wide and pleading and the ghost's are as vicious as icicles.

I get one glimpse before Franklin swings his iron poker at the ghost. It vanishes before contact is made, and Alice slumps to the floor, gasping. The ghost reappears a second later, inches from Franklin. He swings again, and it flickers to a different location, teeth bared like an angry dog.

Helen races to Corinne, grabs her hands, and pulls her upright, while Teddy climbs out from under the baby crib. But when the three of them run for the door, an unseen force lifts them off their feet and hurls them backward. Helen and Teddy sprawl headlong and skid across the floor, and I gasp at the sound of Corinne's head thunking against a wall. Meanwhile, Franklin plays blindman's buff with the actual ghost, except that he isn't blindfolded; he just can't predict where it will appear. His swings are wild and about as effective as swatting at a hornet.

I want to help them, but something holds me back. No one who's entered the nursery seems able to get back out. I watch Teddy try *twice*, only to be assaulted by the crib before he can make it to the doorway. Helen manages to get a stunned Corinne on her feet and tuck her under an arm for support, but they make no further progress. They stand with their heads down and feet spread apart as if buffeted by invisible winds. Franklin keeps swinging his poker, defending Alice, but the ghost stretches its arms to an impossible length, trying to wrap its fingers around her throat again, while Alice sobs on the floor, one hand weakly raised in defense.

"Eleanor!" Helen wails. My knees knock together, and my breathing deafens me. But if I go into that room, I'll be trapped with the rest of them. There has to be another way . . .

We're Roosevelts, after all.

"Cooper Bluff!" I yell. "Make a chain!" Tossing the fireplace shovel aside, I wrap one arm around the doorjamb, straddle the threshold, and stretch out my other hand to Helen.

Her fingers brush mine; our hands join. Then Helen swings Corinne in my direction, like she's the tail on the end of Crack the Whip. Corinne staggers against me, stumbling out of the room. She looks dazed from the blow to her head, and I ask her worriedly, "Can you make it downstairs on your own? You need to get out of this house!"

But Corinne plants herself beside me, linking her arm through mine to become the new anchor of the chain. Her eyes convey the Roosevelt family stubbornness. "We stand or fall together, just like Uncle Theodore says."

Helen grabs Teddy next, deftly inserting him between herself and me. This enables me and Corinne to back up a few steps so that Corinne reaches the top of the staircase. "My—my spectacles," Teddy stammers. He has lost them in the struggle.

"They can be replaced!" Helen snaps. "You can't!"

I no longer have a view into the nursery, but Helen yells through the doorway, "Franklin! Give her to me!"

Alice is thrust out the door. Like Corinne, she's battered and disoriented. Helen passes her to Teddy, who steadies her and pushes her toward me.

Ice crystals explode in the air, pelting us with tiny shards. Alice throws both arms around my neck just as something yanks her backward. I grab her, digging my fingers into her clothing as best I can without unlocking arms with Corinne and Teddy. Alice hangs on to me, and over her shoulder, I lock eyes with the ghost.

Its gaze is that of a prehistoric monster. A dinosaur. A shark. It strikes me to the core with its soulless, predatory intensity. My ears fill with a scratching noise.

Mine. Mine. Mine.

No, that's not it.

Mine to kill. Mine to kill. Mine to kill.

There comes another yank, wrenching Alice away from me and toward the staircase. Her foot slips off the top step. I *see* her lose her balance, and I *try* to free my arms, to catch her before she topples headfirst and backward down the marble stairs. But I can't.

Another explosion of white envelops us, and for the second time I'm hit in the face. I taste the crystals in my mouth. Salt.

Helen has thrown the bag of salt at us.

The ghost splinters into ribbons of fog.

Corinne catches Alice by the hand, and the weight and inertia of our chain are enough to rescue her from the brink of falling.

"We're all out!" Franklin shouts. "Start down the stairs, but don't let go of anyone!"

Salt or no salt, the ghost isn't finished with us. It doesn't physically manifest again, but I feel it in every blast of arctic wind, every icy stab that jolts its way through my bones.

Corinne puts Alice between herself and me, and we *try* to support her. Corinne is nearly as badly injured as Alice, and Alice, our strong, bold, unflappable Alice, weeps brokenly.

My foot slips on the salt-covered marble. Corinne and Teddy compensate for my unbalanced weight. Helen pulls on the chain from above, trying to keep me from falling.

Below us, the front doors fly open so hard, they bounce against the walls.

Shouts. Orders. Men.

They're wearing a light chain mail over their uniforms, which marks them as a SWAT squadron: *Supernatural Weapons and Tactics*. They rush up the stairs, two of them scooping up Alice and Corinne and carrying them down and out the doors, past a moon-faced George gaping at us from the front stoop. Another man fires a salt cannon, spraying the entire staircase. Other officers rush past me. One stops and looks me up and down. Instead of sweeping me into his arms the way the others did Corinne and Alice, he says, "You look like a sturdy girl. Are you harmed in any way?"

I look down at myself. "No," I tell him, rather surprised. I'm covered in salt and ice crystals, but there's not a scratch on me.

He takes me by the elbow. "Then you're the one who's going to tell me what happened here."

21

ALICE LEARNS THE TRUTH, PART TWO

*A*LICE can't stop shivering. Worse, she can't stop crying.

Stop it. You don't behave like this. You're Alice Roosevelt!

But that thought only generates a vivid memory of the voice inside her head.

Kill you, Alice.

The SWAT squadron commandeers a neighboring house to treat the victims of the attack. Officers bundle Alice in blankets and warm compresses. They ask questions, their voices muffled in her ears, and she shakes her head, wanting them to leave her alone. This seems to worry them, so they make Eleanor sit beside her for comfort.

Tears leak down Alice's face in a steady stream while she stares numbly at her surroundings. It's as if everything is happening on the other side of a glass. Alice is grateful for that glass. She wishes she could wrap it around herself and feel nothing ever again.

Franklin and Corinne are being treated for injuries in the next room. A boy wrapped in a scarf with goggles on his head flutters around Helen. Alice belatedly recognizes him as that young man from the séance, George. It seems he's the one who summoned authorities to rescue them from the house. Teddy sits opposite Alice, wrapped in a blanket and missing his spectacles as he explains to the ranking officer why he and Corinne entered the house in the first place.

"We only meant to look through the windows. But we heard a baby crying inside. We thought—somehow—the ghost had gotten hold of a baby. We broke into the house to save it. We followed the cries to the nursery, and the crib was empty. There was no baby. Then *she* appeared. Sissy's mother." Teddy's eyes wander across the room to Alice. "That was your mother, wasn't it, Sissy?"

Alice doesn't answer.

"She went after Corinne first," Teddy continues, "but when Sissy came into the room, the ghost went straight for her."

Of course it went straight for Alice. Her darling daughter. *Kill you, Alice.*

One SWAT man turns to another and says, "That Unsafe notice is over a decade old. If the Vengeful is this strong after all that time—and it's taken to luring victims inside—that house needs to come down. It's a menace."

The owners of *this* house grunt in agreement. They're

an older man and woman, gray-haired and white-faced. Although they didn't object when the SWAT squadron invaded their home, they stand in a corner and make no attempt to help. The blankets and compresses were provided by the police. The residents have not offered so much as hot tea to their half-frozen visitors.

"That house belongs to Commissioner Roosevelt," the senior officer tells the junior one. The younger officer drops his eyes, chastised.

Alice's father isn't "Commissioner Roosevelt" anymore and hasn't been for a couple of years. But these men still feel loyal to the former head of the city police force.

"You mean these are his children?" one of the other young officers asks in a whisper. "The ghost's progenitor was his . . ." He gives a low whistle.

The entire police force will know by nightfall. If they don't already. How did Alice's father manage to keep this scandal a secret during his term on the Police Commission? Theodore Roosevelt's first wife produced a powerful Vengeful ghost in the heart of Manhattan. It should have made headlines, but the powers that be suppressed it.

The ranking officer addresses Alice: "Where does he live now?"

Alice, behind her glass wall, declines to answer. The officer turns to Teddy. "Where does your father live now, son?"

"Washington, D.C.," Teddy replies, blinking nearsightedly.

"Alice and Teddy have been staying with Uncle Theodore's

sister." Eleanor intervenes. "Mrs. William Cowles, on East Twenty-First Street."

"And the rest of this crowd?" The officer waves a hand at the Roosevelt cousins in the next room.

"The same."

The officer looks pointedly at an underling. "Send someone to warn Mrs. Cowles to expect a passel of frost-burned youngsters arriving on her doorstep in the next half hour."

"Please, sir." Eleanor pops up like a jack-in-the-box to catch the officer's attention before he moves on to other matters. "There's a lady living in Number Four, Miss Barnstable. I visited her last week, and she didn't seem in her right mind. Her house is next to Number Six . . ."

The officer addresses the residents of this house. "Are you familiar with Miss Barnstable?"

The gray-haired gentleman frowns. "Only vaguely. We keep to ourselves on this street."

The SWAT officer gives the man a disparaging look. "We'll check on her, miss," he tells Eleanor, indicating with his tone that the neighbors should have done so before now.

They're unhinged. Alice stares at the carpet. *My mother's ghost turned the inhabitants of this street into madwomen and hermits.*

She shudders violently, and Eleanor puts an arm around her. "Won't you speak to me?" Eleanor asks quietly. "Please say something, Alice."

Alice shrugs. What is there to say?

When the police escort them to carriages, Alice has a

chance to see the damage done to her cousins. Corinne has bruises around her neck that correspond to Alice's. Franklin has several frost burns. As far as Alice can see, Helen has come away unscathed, except that she can't get rid of George, who seems to think he saved her life.

The confusion in the entryway to Aunt Bye's house— SWAT officers, the cousins, a doctor who was summoned— allows Alice to slip upstairs without speaking to her aunt. Just as her feet disappear from sight below, she hears Aunt Bye call out. "Alice!"

She doesn't stop.

Footsteps follow her. Not Aunt Bye's but Eleanor's recognizable clomps. Alice slips into her room without looking back but leaves the door slightly ajar. Eleanor's presence is . . . acceptable. Crossing the room, Alice lays the photograph facedown on her bedside table with a snap.

Golden curls. Blue-gray eyes. A little bow mouth.

Alice's skin crawls as if it's trying to shrug its way off her bones.

Eleanor closes the door and, without saying anything, goes straight to Alice's dresser. She pulls out the thickest, heaviest undergarments she can find, then turns her attention to Alice's wardrobe. Alice almost speaks at that point. *That shirtwaist doesn't match that skirt!* But her cousin's choices do look warm, and speaking is too much effort. It's all she can do to start unfastening the clothes she has on.

When Alice is dressed in dry, warm clothes, Eleanor unpins her cousin's hair and brushes it out. "I want my snake," Alice says abruptly, and Eleanor fetches Emily Spinach. Or rather, she fetches the box and lets Alice pick up the snake. Eleanor goes back to brushing hair while Alice strokes her pet.

Blue-gray eyes. A little bow mouth. Ice-cold hands—squeezing.

A gentle knock precedes Aunt Bye's entrance by only a second. "Eleanor, give us a moment." Eleanor nods and walks out, and Aunt Bye stands over Alice, her hands folded across her rounded stomach. "What I told you about your family before was mostly truth. But it wasn't all of the truth."

Alice doesn't acknowledge this outrageous understatement.

"Your mother died unexpectedly. My mother was ill with typhoid fever, your father was as distraught as I've ever seen him, and you were a tiny infant." Aunt Bye pauses, then continues as if the words have to be forced from her mouth. "Two days after your mother's death, that ghost erupted. *Two days* of dormancy is extremely rare—almost unheard of. It smothered my mother in her sleep." Her voice breaks, becomes gravel in her throat. "It tried to smother you. Theodore and I surely would've been next, but we awoke in time, rescued you, and fled the house."

Alice manages to say with only a slight tremor, "That house should be demolished. I heard the SWAT squadron saying so."

"Your father wouldn't allow it. But after this . . . When he hears how it attacked you and Teddy and Corinne— believe me, the house will come down."

Will it? Alice isn't convinced. The ghost killed his mother and tried to kill his infant daughter, and Father did nothing but close up the house.

"Will you forgive me, Alice? For not telling you before?"

Alice answers immediately. "Of course. This wasn't your secret to tell. It was *his*." Her aunt opens her mouth, probably to defend her brother—as she always does—but Alice briskly changes the subject. "Now, will you leave *this* house? Please? Until the baby is born? After what happened today . . ."

"That has nothing to do with this house. As I told you, I feel more comfortable giving birth here." Aunt Bye glances left and right, as if Alice might be hiding listeners in her wardrobe or behind her dresser. "*He* says it's more important than ever that I stay."

Alice's heart thumps. They've almost completely emptied the attic and Davy is still whispering to her aunt?

Another knock, and the door opens wide enough for Ida's face. "Mrs. Cowles, there are reporters here."

"I'll be right there, Ida." Aunt Bye runs an affectionate hand over Alice's head, smoothing her hair. "Take the time you need, darling, then please join us downstairs."

Alice nods, although she doesn't intend to go downstairs. Aunt Bye leaves, but the door is caught by a slim hand before it closes. Teddy peeks in. "Are you all right, Sissy?"

She nods.

Teddy takes that as permission to enter and walks over to her. He squints at the overturned photograph and then at Alice. "I wanted to say—that thing at the house today, it wasn't your mother."

It was.

"I know I said that to the police . . ." He gulps. "I shouldn't have. I'm really sorry. That ghost is just a *thing* that got left behind from her death. You shouldn't blame your mother."

"Why not? Everyone else does." Alice swallows but can't dislodge the bitterness coating her tongue. "No one even calls me by my name because it was hers. Not Father, not you, not Mother Edith . . ."

Teddy's mouth drops open. "We *do*. Of course we call you Alice, but not when you're around. We use *Sissy* because we thought hearing your mother's name made you sad."

"Alice is *my* name." She means to state it as a matter of fact, but it comes out as a wail.

Teddy cringes, then lifts his chin and stiffens his spine in a way that evokes their father's image. "That's true. Consider it noted." And—daft and impulsive as her brother is—Alice knows he will never call her Sissy again. "Now, about this." He turns the photograph of her mother upright.

"I can't look at that!" Alice turns her face away.

Burning fingers. Cutting off her air.

"Then I'll take it and put it by *my* bed. Because this is how you should remember your mother. That thing . . . It's unfair that it stole her face, but you know it's not your mother. Your mother *loved* you, and if you can't look at her right now, then I will. I'll remember her for you until you're ready."

Teddy picks up the photograph and takes a few steps toward the door before peering nearsightedly back at her.

If he's expecting her to ask for the portrait back, he's mistaken. Alice says nothing.

You Are Cordially Invited

to a Soirée

with Music, Billiards, Charades,

and Other Amusements and Refreshments

at the Home of Mrs. William Cowles

Hosted by Helen Roosevelt

February 24, 1898

at Seven O'Clock

132 East 21st Street,

New York, New York

22

ELEANOR AT THE PARTY

IF anyone were to ask me, I'd say the last thing we need is a party at Aunt Bye's house. But according to Franklin, Helen becomes distraught when anyone suggests that she cancel it.

"It's unlike Helen. She acts as if her entire social"—Franklin gropes for a word—"*queendom* will collapse if she doesn't host this party. Aunt Bye is willing as long as Alice is comfortable with it. And Alice says she's perfectly fine."

Perfectly fine. That's what Alice tells everyone who asks how she is. I'm worried for her. Alice has put up a wall to prevent us from seeing how badly hurt she really is.

Corinne, by contrast, behaves the way one would expect. She cried and hugged me and thanked me for coming to her rescue. She has told the story of her encounter with the ghost over and over, to everyone who will listen, as if each retelling puts her further from the horror of the actual event until it is simply something scary that once happened to her. Perhaps even something to brag about. *I survived a Vengeful!* Teddy is much the same, although he talks less about his adventure, probably out of deference to his sister.

When I try with Alice, however, she refuses to discuss it. The one time I pressed her on the subject, she pulled that snake from her pocket and dangled it in my face. "Do you want to hold Emily Spinach?"

I recoiled, although not as much as I once would have. "Not really."

Alice nodded with satisfaction. "That's how much I feel like talking about it." She put her snake back in her pocket, and I stopped asking questions.

I regret that I ever wished to see my father and brother as ghosts. For the first time I understand why Grandmother Hall hides in her room to avoid Uncle Valentine on the stairs—and why, if she had any inkling about the ghost that drove the Roosevelts from their house on Fifty-Seventh Street, it was something she chose never to gossip about. I understand why Uncle Will was worried that the presence of both Alice and a ghost in the house would bring back horrifying memories for his expectant wife.

And I think of Gracie, who was so young when the rest of our family died that he has only photographs instead of memories. I would not want those images tarnished by what Alice saw in her old nursery.

The portrait of Alice's mother, I notice, is no longer on her bedside table.

Two days before her party, Helen arrives on my doorstep. "I'm here to take you dress shopping."

Like a spider hidden in a web that only reveals itself when the fly gets tangled, Grandmother sails into the hallway. "Good day, Nancy," she says coldly.

"Helen," I correct her.

"Thank you for your invitation," Grandmother continues, not caring what her name is. "But Eleanor does not have the funds to procure a new dress for every occasion, nor do I, with an entire house to maintain, have it within my means to provide it."

"It's my pleasure, Mrs. Hall," Helen says. "I'll buy the dress."

Grandmother shakes her head. "That's charity."

"Then please," Helen persists, "may Eleanor come to help me choose *my* dress?"

Grandmother's eyes light up at the cruelty of that suggestion. "She may. If only to comprehend the frivolity of such an expenditure."

Helen seizes my arm before I can beg off. Only after we are on our way does she explain. "The money for your dress comes from Alice."

"What?"

"Her stepmother sent the money as a dress allowance for Alice, but she gave it to me to use for you." Helen eyes me slyly. "Come now, Eleanor. Don't you want to look nice for . . ."

"For whom?" I demand.

Helen shrugs innocently. "Don't turn this down. You know how Alice has been since *the incident*. If it makes her feel better to buy you a gift, won't you allow it?"

And that is how I end up with the scarlet dress. I choose something pale blue. Helen overrules me. The dressmaker takes my measurements for alteration, and we order that the dress be delivered to Aunt Bye's house so Grandmother won't know.

On the evening of the party, I leave home in something *she* considers suitable and change into my new ensemble at Aunt Bye's. Helen supervises my transformation, Corinne obeys her commands, and Alice watches. I'd thank her for the dress if she would acknowledge the gift, but Alice keeps up her pretense that it is nothing to do with her. When Helen declares me "finished," they finally let me look in a mirror to see the whole effect, and I gasp out loud.

The skirt and sleeves are made of scarlet velvet, and the bodice is black silk embroidered with white and gold roses. Helen and Corinne have loosely piled most of my hair on top of my head, but they left some hanging down my back, curled into ringlets.

"Eleanor, you could pass for sixteen," Helen says, admiring her handiwork.

Corinne hugs me, very gently so as not to rumple the dress. "You're beautiful!"

I look at her beaming face—and then at Helen—and I know with one hundred percent certainty that the cruel conversation I overheard on the day of their arrival never happened. It was an auditory hallucination, courtesy of the rotten, mischievous Davy. I turn back to the mirror and smile.

"Eleanor," snaps Alice, "for goodness' sake, take your hand away from your mouth!"

I drop my hand, flushing in embarrassment, but Alice is right. I don't need to cover my mouth to look pretty. Not tonight.

Having finished with me, the other girls get dressed. I help with their hair, wielding the curling tongs and only burning myself once. Corinne wears an extra-large bow for the occasion, and Helen chooses her best jewelry. Alice puts her snake in her pocket. After we have bedecked and becurled everyone to our satisfaction, we head downstairs.

Helen has spent the whole day decorating with party streamers and paper snowflakes. Ida's two younger sisters, who aren't much older than I am, have been hired as extra help, and the three of them are busily laying out the food in the dining room. Immediately, Helen rushes in to interfere, rearranging the placement of the dishes and criticizing their choice of serving platters.

"Hello, Eleanor. That dress is very pretty." I turn around to find Franklin smiling at me.

"Helen picked it out," I say, automatically deflecting the compliment.

He raises his eyebrows. "Do you not like it?"

I smile. Raise my hand. Lower it. "No. I do like it."

"Have you heard from Miss Bly?"

My smile fades. "No."

I wrote Nellie Bly after I found the insurance policies, explaining my suspicions. I thought I would hear back . . . "I know she is busy, and it seems as if the ghost has faded since you cleared the attic. I suppose it's not urgent anymore."

"Do you think you might be wrong? I can see a wife poisoning her husband—although I don't commend it in general practice—but a mother murdering her children? For insurance money?"

Franklin wants to believe it is a coincidence, the policies and the deaths, but it's not. "You saw the dates," I say. Every policy was purchased between one and two years before the person's death and in the exact order in which they would die.

I've been to the library since I discovered the horrible truth. I read about Mary Ann Cotton, an English woman who poisoned multiple husbands and children for their life insurance, and Lydia Sherman, who did the same thing in Connecticut. In both cases, it seemed to be a murderous compulsion, because neither woman *needed* the money. They simply *wanted* it. I look Franklin in the eyes. "There are things that can grip a person even more strongly than love of family. For my father, it was alcohol. For Mrs. Drummond, it must have been money."

Franklin drops his eyes and looks ashamed that he broached this subject, which was not my intention. Luckily, the doorbell rings, rescuing us from an awkward moment.

The house fills with guests. They're Helen's age, and I

don't know any of them except for George, who drove the motorcar. A few boys try to talk to me, but mostly I flee from them before they discover I'm hardly older than Corinne. She and Teddy, so much younger than the guests, slink around the outskirts of the party, watching and giggling and acting as if this is another adventure, far less harrowing than their last.

Alice has no trouble fitting in. She plays billiards with the boys and talks fashion with the girls. There's no sign of the girl who was carried four days ago, limp and sobbing, out of the house haunted by her mother.

Several guests ask about Aunt Bye, who has sent apologies for being indisposed and promises to make an appearance later.

Eventually, the guests settle into various amusements. Some play billiards. Others divide into teams for charades. Helen, however, does not seem satisfied. She flits around, rearranging the food, nudging guests here or there. I follow her with my eyes, wondering what, exactly, is preventing her from enjoying her own party.

George has brought a gramophone and three recorded discs in an effort to impress Helen. He sets the gramophone up in the parlor and cranks the device himself, playing "Sweet Genevieve," "On the Banks of the Wabash," and "A Hot Time in the Old Town Tonight" over and over and over.

Meanwhile, Helen grabs Ida by the elbow and whispers fiercely in her ear. Ida cringes away from her, speaking respectfully but flinging her free arm out to indicate the offerings on the dining table. Helen is complaining; Ida is defending. When I look at the food on the table, I don't see anything wrong. I also don't see anybody eating.

Franklin's voice in my ear makes me jump. "*The rose of youth was dew-impearled.* What does that *mean?*"

I blink at him idiotically until I realize he's quoting a line from the song playing on the gramophone. "I don't think it means anything. Do you think Helen is acting strange?"

"If George had brought something respectable, I'd ask you to dance. Helen *is* wound up tight, but this party is important to her."

"I don't know how to dance. And why is it more important than any other?"

"I have no idea. I could *teach* you to dance, if you like."

He's looking at me rather intently, and I'm not sure how to respond because he has already said that George's music isn't the right kind for dancing. Before I figure out what to say, something in the dining room draws my attention. Two girls approach the table, then recoil and leave the room in far too much of a hurry. I walk away from Franklin.

"Eleanor?" He follows.

The dining table practically groans with the weight of all the food, most of it untouched. There are roast beef and sliced ham, oysters on the half shell, pâté of goose liver, creamed corn, endives in cream, and an endless variety of cakes and sweetmeats. I pick up a plate, thinking that if one person starts eating, the rest might join in, but no sooner do I reach for a serving fork than everything on the table transforms.

The beef is burned; the ham soaks in congealed fat. The oysters are rancid, the creamed corn curdled. The pâté is riddled with lumps, and all the cakes are streaked with green mold. The stench of spoiled food makes my gorge rise, and I step back, gagging.

Between one blink and the next, everything returns to normal.

"Davy," I say between my teeth. Obviously, the ghost is not as faded as we hoped. He's back to his old tricks. No wonder the guests aren't eating. I turn to Franklin to ask what he sees, but he spins around in alarm as raised voices swell in the billiards room.

Two boys are arguing at the billiards table. One is upset over losing, and the other is demanding payment of a wager between them.

"It's that blasted music that's put me off my game," the loser declares angrily. "I'm putting a stop to it!" Ignoring his opponent's request for the winnings, he hefts the billiard cue over his shoulder and leaves the room by the other door. By the expression on his face, he's on his way to crack that cue over the gramophone, or George's head, or both.

"Hey! Hold up, there!" Franklin exclaims, darting after him.

I mean to follow, but at that moment, Ida walks into the dining room from the direction of the kitchen. She's carrying a sugar bowl and doesn't acknowledge my presence, even though we're the only two people in the room. Walking with an oddly stiff gait, she dumps the sugar into the punch bowl. "Ida?" She doesn't answer. Instead, she uses the ladle to stir the punch. "Ida!" I grab her hand.

The girl jumps and flinches. "Goodness, Miss Eleanor! You startled me!"

"What are you doing?"

Ida looks down. The sugar sinks to the bottom of the punch bowl. If it is sugar. Something about it looks very wrong to me. The crystals are too coarse, too heavy. "What . . . what is that?" Ida stares at the sugar bowl in her hands as if she's never seen it before.

My skin crawls. "I'll take care of it." Picking up the punch bowl, I hold it ahead of me, careful not to splash my dress, and carry it into the kitchen.

In spite of the fact that we have a party underway and there are more servants in the house than usual, the kitchen is empty. There are pots on the stove, plates warming in the oven, and no one watching them. I pour the punch into the sink and rinse the bowl under the faucet, looking nervously around. Where are Maisie and the other two girls? I check the food, make sure nothing is burning or boiling over, and start back to the party.

The door slams shut.

I grab the handle and pull, but the door won't budge. While I struggle, a damp cold falls over the room. Not the biting, clawing cold of the old Roosevelt mansion, but a foul, earthy cold that would emanate from a grave. Dread trickles down the back of my neck, and I turn to see Davy

Drummond's ghost, which reveals itself in a full-body manifestation at last.

I'm facing a boy Teddy's age, with dark brown hair and a thin, foxy face. It wears knee-length trousers over droopy white socks, a plain white shirt, and a short jacket with a single button at the throat. This ghost would look like an ordinary boy in 1850s costume if it weren't clinging like a spider to the wall of the servants' staircase. The sight sends a lightning bolt of panic through every nerve in my body. It's so inhumanly *wrong*.

The ghost smiles at me, and a whisper tickles my ear. "Bye."

Then it scuttles sideways up the staircase wall and out of sight.

I look at the back door, wondering if I can get out of the house that way. But that thing went upstairs, and it wasn't telling me goodbye. It was saying my aunt's name.

❧ 23 ❧

ALICE MEETS A CRACKPOT

𝒜LICE is not enjoying the party as much as she pretends. Pride alone keeps her Alice Act intact—showing off Emily Spinach, complimenting Helen's friends on their dresses. She doesn't know how many of these people have heard the story of what happened at her father's old house, so she makes a point of showing how unaffected she is.

One thing has cheered her today—seeing Eleanor sweep through the house in that gorgeous gown, smiling and swishing her skirts with Franklin trailing lovelorn behind her.

The idea to buy Eleanor a new dress came when Alice's eyes fell upon the letter Mother Edith sent last week. Although she scanned it briefly on the day it arrived, this time, the disparaging remark about Eleanor's clothes jumped out at her. The fleeting flash of rage Alice felt in defense of her cousin surprised her. She promptly asked Aunt Bye for the dress allowance and turned it over to Helen. "Buy something for Eleanor and don't let her know it came from me." It wasn't anonymity she wanted so much as avoiding Eleanor's thanks—and questions. If prodded on why she felt compelled to bestow this gift, Alice might explode and blurt out Mother Edith's heartless comment. And Eleanor doesn't deserve to hear it.

This is what I have for mothers. One Vengeful ghost. And one spiteful second choice.

And Aunt Bye, a stubborn part of her mind reminds her.

When the grating noise of George's gramophone drives her from the parlor and she can't finagle a spot at the billiards table, Alice steps out the front door, hoping to find another distraction. Helen's friends were smoking cigarettes on the stoop earlier, and Alice believes she can talk them into letting her try one, if Helen—or more likely Franklin—isn't around to interfere. But the smoking boys are no longer there.

Alice is about to go back inside when two figures turn from the sidewalk onto the steps leading to Aunt Bye's front door. The first is a woman, and when she looks up, Alice recognizes Nellie Bly. "Miss Roosevelt!" she exclaims. "Well met."

The man behind Miss Bly is tall and thin, with dark hair and a neatly trimmed mustache. He wears a suit and coat that look like garments of quality that have been worn for too many years, and he carries a large, bulky case that sparks Alice's curiosity. "Good evening, Miss Bly. We weren't sure if we were going to hear from you again."

Miss Bly mounts to the top step and beams at Alice from beneath another stunning hat. "I wanted to be in touch after I consulted my expert, and here he is. Alice Roosevelt, may I introduce you to the world's most talented inventor, Mr. Nikola Tesla!"

"Never heard of him," Alice says suspiciously, remembering that Miss Bly also said her expert friend was a bit of a crackpot.

Miss Bly's eyebrows shoot up. "*It is tact that is golden, not silence. Samuel Butler.*"

Alice's cheeks burn. Tact is not her strongest quality. She *should* make an effort at manners for someone who has come here to help. "I'm sorry, Mr. Tesla. Thank you for coming." The gentleman doesn't seem to have taken offense. He surveys Alice with a pair of eyes that are sharp and keen and might very well see straight through her. Self-consciously, she opens the front door and escorts the guests inside.

In the foyer, Miss Bly looks at the streamers and snowflakes and the coatracks overflowing with garments. "What's happening here?"

"It's a party."

Mr. Tesla surveys the house as seriously as he did Alice moments ago, and Alice has the impression that he's looking beyond the decorations and furniture to the bones of the structure itself. At least, until a raucous screech blurts from the gramophone in the parlor. *That* household item gets his attention, and he grimaces. "Is there someplace quiet where I can work?"

Alice beckons the ex-journalist and the inventor down the hall toward Aunt Bye's sitting room. Along the way, she keeps an eye out for a scarlet dress, knowing Eleanor will be interested in what these two have to say, but she doesn't see Eleanor before they reach the sitting room. Once inside, Mr. Tesla closes the door with a sigh of relief. "Some inventions are created for the betterment of humankind," he murmurs, "and others merely to disturb the peace."

"Now, now," Miss Bly chastises him before turning to Alice. "Mr. Tesla has a rather unusual theory about ghost eruptions. He believes that the progenitor of a ghost is not the *person* who died, but the *house* in which the person died."

"That's crazy!" Alice says, reflecting a moment too late on silence and tact.

Again, Mr. Tesla doesn't seem offended. He removes a potted fern and two china figurines from one of Aunt Bye's side tables, pulls the table into the center of the room, and sets his case upon it. "Death leaves an impression on a house," he says, unbuckling the case and folding open various compartments. "This impression can fester and grow over a period of days, months, or years before erupting into a supernatural occurrence. The emotions released in a house—dread, anger, and grief—by the dying *and* the bereaved have a great impact on whether that house will subsequently become haunted." He lifts glass tubes out of the case and screws them into other places. "People underestimate the contribution of the bereaved. Intense grief can result in violent apparitions." Mr. Tesla bends a wire contraption shaped like a Y into a vertical position.

"This house has a tragic history," Nellie Bly says reflectively. "A chronic illness took the family members one by one over a period of a decade. I assume the accumulated dread of the occupants, the drawn-out sicknesses, the waiting and fear about who would be next made this a very unpleasant place to live. And prone to an eruption."

Alice shakes her head throughout Miss Bly's account. "No, no—that's not how it happened at all. Didn't you get Eleanor's letter?"

"I did not see one. I don't usually open my own mail."

Alice explains about the life insurance policies and how they mirror the order in which the Drummond family members died. Even Nellie Bly, who saw cruelty firsthand in state-run asylums, sinks into one of the chairs with a hand to her heart. "Monstrous."

Mr. Tesla is more pragmatic. "This house has witnessed dreadful things."

"So did Davy Drummond." Alice is not convinced that ghosts can be produced by houses. It would be more *comforting* to think that her mother's Vengeful ghost originated from a brick-and-mortar house and her father's overwhelming grief instead of the woman who birthed her. But that wouldn't make it true. "Does anyone else share your theory, Mr. Tesla?"

"Not many," he replies. "It has been rejected quite famously, several times. The psychologist Dr. William James discounted it because houses have no souls. Mr. Thomas Edison dismissed it as irrelevant. He said it does not matter where ghosts come from since our main priority is to detect, deter, and diminish them."

"Doesn't that make you angry?" Alice asks. "Having your theories rejected?"

"Why should it? Theories must be tested—and rejected if they do not stand the test of proof. On the path to that proof, I believe in collecting all possible data." Tesla switches on his device. The bent wire begins to rotate. The glass tubes glow.

"What is that?" Alice wants to know.

"A spirit telegraph," Miss Bly says jokingly.

"It's a means of hearing what the house has to say," Tesla corrects her. Leaning over his equipment, he adjusts various dials. The antenna twitches left and right. The machine crackles and buzzes. Tesla glances at the door. "Ignore the distractions, if you can."

There are plenty of distractions to ignore. George's gramophone. The crack of cues on billiard balls. Girls' laughter. And then Alice lifts her head like a hunting dog on the scent. Something thrums through Mr. Tesla's machine.

Claws scrape on wood, and hair swishes against plaster— the sound of mice in the walls. Tesla adjusts one of the antennas. Wind batters against the doors; branches scratch the windows; floorboards expand and contract. Alice glances at the inventor. These are ordinary house sounds, nothing to do with the supernatural.

Mr. Tesla turns more dials. "We must delve deeper."

More static—and then something like a sob comes from

the machine. Heavy breathing. A whimper. Alice turns toward Nellie Bly. "How do we know these sounds aren't coming from someone inside the house now?"

"Shhh." Miss Bly's brow tenses in concentration.

A moan is followed by harsh retching—the sound of someone violently expelling the contents of their stomach. Bile rises in Alice's throat.

Then, an enticing whisper. *Drink your tea.*

"Nikola," Miss Bly murmurs.

This time, Mr. Tesla is the one to say "Shhhh."

Drink. Your. Tea. The words repeat, coldly, with no emotion.

Tea. Alice grasps at a memory. Why is that familiar?

At the séance, George asked, *How did you die?* And a dead rat appeared on the table.

Then Alice asked, *What else do you want to tell us?* And the pendulum swung to *T . . . T . . . T . . . T . . .*

"Drink your tea!"

Alice flinches at the malice in this third and most chilling repetition of the command. "It was the tea! That's how she poisoned them. Rat poison in the tea!"

Tesla shakes his head grimly. "These are not the sounds of a Friendly haunting."

"It can't be an Unaware," Miss Bly says. "They don't interact with new inhabitants in any meaningful way, and this one has."

"The sounds of an Unaware haunting are detached and disjointed." Tesla points at his machine. "This house is telling a story, and a gruesome one at that. If these young people knew or suspected they were being poisoned, imagine the fear and the dread that would build up in this dwelling. That points to a Vengeful haunting."

"But a Vengeful would have attacked by now. It probably would have attacked on the first day." Miss Bly's eyes are alight with excitement. "Are you saying this is something different? An entirely new category?"

"Not necessarily," Tesla demurs. "It is more likely an outlier, a haunting with characteristics far removed from the normative. In every category—Friendly, Unaware, Vengeful—it is possible to find outliers. The debate over whether the ghost of Abraham Lincoln was an Unaware or a Friendly is almost certainly because it too was an outlier. There are other, less famous examples—"

Alice interrupts his impromptu lesson in diagnostics. "What does it mean for *this* house? Are we in danger here?"

Tesla holds up a hand once more, signaling them to be quiet. Alice assumes he has heard something more from his machine, but he turns it off with a brisk *click* and faces the closed door. "There are a lot of people in this house today."

"It's a party," Alice repeats. Then she hears what has caught the inventor's attention—a cascade of voices on the other side of the door. Not the usual merriment of a social gathering, but words of anger. A shout, followed by a great crash. Hurrying around Mr. Tesla, Alice throws open the door.

Partygoers are gathered in the entranceway to the

parlor, straining to see over one another's shoulders. Franklin's voice rises above the tumult. "Put it down, I tell you!"

Tesla follows Alice into the hall. "Hauntings can gather strength from the response of the living, and when there is a great congregation of people and high emotion, the situation may escalate exponentially."

"I don't understand what you're saying," Alice complains.

"I am saying it would be wise to evacuate the house."

24

ELEANOR BESIEGED

THE second floor is icebox cold, but I see no sign of Davy Drummond on the walls or ceiling. My skin still crawls from the sight of his ghost skittering up the stairwell.

I burst into my aunt's room without bothering to knock. My racing heart jolts faster because she is sitting upright in her bed, both arms clasped over her stomach, grimacing in pain. "Aunt Bye!"

She's wearing a nightdress, and her hair is plaited in one long braid. Despite what she said earlier, she obviously never meant to come down to the party. Looking up at me, she is as helpless as a child. "Eleanor, I think I'm going into labor."

It's too soon. *Months* too soon.

"Lie down!" I exclaim. "Put your feet up!" As if gravity will stop the baby from coming.

But Aunt Bye obeys. "Please," she mutters under her

breath, hands pressed against her stomach. "You promised me. You promised me."

Who promised her? Is she speaking to the baby? To God? Or to the ghost that whispered her baby would be born healthy if she stayed in this house? "I'll summon a doctor." I swivel toward the door, but before I get there my eyes fall upon a teacup on her nightstand. Alarm bells ring in my head. "Aunt Bye, where did this tea come from?"

She gazes at me with troubled eyes. "I don't know. I dozed off, and it was here when I awoke. I assume Maisie brought it."

That's possible. But I'm remembering the odd-looking sugar Ida poured into the punch bowl. And the questionable sugar I found the time the ghost offered me tea. It occurs to me that on the morning after the eruption, the diagnosis of Friendly was decided because the ghost offered the investigators cups of tea—*and the sugar bowl.*

"Did you drink any of this?" My voice comes out shrill.

"I—I'm not sure," Aunt Bye stammers. "A sip or two, maybe." She curls into herself, gripping her stomach and stiffening. "Ohhhh."

Is she really in labor? Or has she been poisoned? Ella Drummond killed her victims *somehow,* and the ghost has been showing us, over and over, these cups of tea. "Don't touch any more of it." I pick up the cup to take it away.

A swarm of cockroaches crawls out of the cup and over my hand. I shriek and let go. China shatters on the ground,

spraying tea everywhere. Of course, there are no cockroaches now.

"Eleanor?" Aunt Bye looks so confused, so helpless. She
tries to sit up.

"Don't get up. I'll tell Maisie to fetch a doctor and be
right back." The bedroom door is closed, although I don't
remember shutting it, and when I reach for the handle, the
cockroaches reappear. They cover the doorknob. Closing my
eyes, I grab the knob anyway. I feel their twitchy legs crawl-
ing over my skin, but I don't let go.

The knob won't turn.

I twist as hard as I can using both hands, and it doesn't
budge. My eyes fly open. "Where's the key to the door?"

"I don't think there is one. We never lock it. Eleanor,
what's happening?"

I bang on the door with the heel of my hand. "The ghost
locked us in!"

"Why would it do that?"

My poor aunt still thinks this ghost is a Friendly.
"Maisie!" I yell, pounding on the door with both fists. "Anyone! Help! We need help!"

Abandoning the locked door, I dash to one of the windows facing the front of the house and force the latches
open. But the sash won't go up, no matter how I yank on it.
I look down, hoping to see the boys who were smoking on
the front step earlier. To my surprise, guests are leaving the
house in a stream, pulling on coats and hats as they go—and

if I am not mistaken, that is Nellie Bly waving them out. I smack my hand on the glass and shout. No one hears or sees me.

Thankfully, a muffled voice calls out from the second-floor hallway. "Aunt Bye!" Urgent knocking shakes the door.

"Franklin?" Darting back across the room, I rattle the doorknob and shout, "Aunt Bye needs a doctor, but the ghost locked us in!"

"Eleanor? Stand back from the door!" Franklin says something that sounds like *"Will you help me, sir?"* and I step back as the door shudders. An image comes to mind of my cousin throwing his shoulder against the door, like a hero in a novel, but the blows come from much lower. He's kicking it, which is smarter *and* effective. The latch breaks, and the door flies open.

Franklin stumbles into the room. With him is a tall gentleman I have never seen before. Aunt Bye clutches the bedsheets to her chin and stares at them in distress. "She needs a doctor," I repeat.

"Get something warm on her," Franklin says. "We'll take her to a hospital."

Throwing open my aunt's wardrobe, I search for something to put on. "What is happening downstairs?"

"Miss Bly arrived with Mr. Tesla here, who says the house must be evacuated."

"Evacuated?" Aunt Bye repeats as I wrap a thick dressing gown around her and help to put her arms through the sleeves.

I don't know who this Mr. Tesla is, but I cannot argue with his good sense. "Can you stand?" I slip my arm around my aunt, and Franklin does the same on the other side. We get her to her feet and help her a few steps toward the door, where she doubles over, clasping her stomach. My eyes meet Franklin's over her head, and the same thought flashes between us. If the baby comes tonight, it will not survive.

Alice skids into the doorway. "Everyone is out except us." She stares. "What's wrong with Aunt Bye?"

"We'll take her to the hospital," Franklin says again, trying to sound calm. "Everything will be all right." As soon as our aunt's spasm passes, Franklin and I get her moving again. Her feet are bare, I realize, and I glance around frantically, looking for shoes or slippers. Instead, I see the bedroom door swinging shut.

"The door!"

Mr. Tesla leaps forward and catches it. He firmly holds it open while Franklin and I half-drag, half-carry Aunt Bye out.

Alice, in the hall, starts repeatedly stamping her feet.

"What are you doing?" Franklin demands, but I guess even before Alice explains.

"Cockroaches! Don't you see them?"

Suddenly we do. Legions of cockroaches, swarming toward us. Aunt Bye recoils and tries to pull away from us. "They're an illusion!" Mr. Tesla says, his voice soft but urgent. "Keep moving!"

Then an electric lamp mounted on the corridor wall

flares and pops. The wallpaper blackens in a straight line to the next lamp, which, in turn, flares. The glass globe shatters, and the black line grows along the wall. With dread, I remember Grandmother's dire prediction. *Electric lights! Mark my words. Your aunt will be lucky if her entire family doesn't burn up in an electrical fire!*

"It's another illusion." Alice sounds more hopeful than certain.

It's not an illusion. We smell the smoke.

"On behalf of those of us at the back of the ranks," says Franklin, "I urge you to keep moving."

When we reach the head of the staircase, however, Mr. Tesla throws out an arm in warning, bringing us to a stop. The stairs aren't there. Instead, the first-floor foyer gapes ten feet below us.

Mr. Tesla takes only a second to survey the situation. "*That* is another illusion. There's no wreckage." He turns to address Aunt Bye. "Madam, will you trust me?"

My poor aunt, terrified and in pain, nods.

Mr. Tesla replaces me at her side and lifts Aunt Bye into his arms. Franklin helps him secure his hold on her before the gentleman turns toward the nonexistent staircase. Alice and I clutch each other as he steps into the abyss.

They do not pitch into space and fall. Mr. Tesla's feet land firmly on the invisible treads of the stairs. Within seconds, he makes it to the first floor and carries Aunt Bye toward the door.

Franklin steps to the head of the staircase, positioning

himself in front of me and Alice. "We can do the same. I'll lead you down." He holds out his hand to me, and I take it. I reach for Alice, but she stares past us.

"Franklin!" she warns.

He looks. I look. The fire has followed the wiring across the stairwell ceiling to the chandelier hanging over the staircase. Bulbs flare, shattering glass. At the same moment, the ceiling around the fixture crumbles. The chandelier drops, its wires swinging it in an arc toward the second-floor landing like a wrecking ball. Toward us.

"Run, girls!" Franklin shouts, pushing me back the way we came.

We whirl around and pelt in retreat down the second-floor hallway. Alice sprints into the lead. I have barely started running when there's a sickening thud behind me. Something hits my back, carrying me forward and knocking me to the floor. Briefly, I'm pinned to the ground, but panic gives me the strength to crawl out from under the dead weight. After dragging my skirt free, I wriggle around to discover that the dead weight is Franklin.

He's sprawled on the hallway floor, unconscious, the back of his head bloodied from the blow of the chandelier, shards of glass everywhere.

Around us, the walls burn.

25

ALICE IN THE FLAMES

WHILE Eleanor hunches over Franklin, calling his name and blotting his bleeding head with the skirt of her dress, Alice surveys the staircase. It's visible now but showered in broken glass, plaster, and pieces of the chandelier. They won't be escaping in that direction. Which leaves the servants' stairs.

"There's only one way out." Alice hooks her hands under one of Franklin's arms. Eleanor does the same, and together they manage to heave him a couple of feet down the hall. "Why is your beau such a big, heavy lunk?" Alice complains. Such is Eleanor's distress that she doesn't even bother to refute the word *beau*. "How are we going to get him down the stairs? Roll him like a sack of potatoes?"

Luckily, Franklin chooses that moment to groan and flounder about. "Franklin!" Eleanor exclaims. "Can you hear me?"

"More importantly," interjects Alice, "can you stand?"

He stands by degrees, getting onto his hands and knees and then dragging himself to his feet. He sways, one hand going to the back of his head and coming away bloody.

"Lean on me." Eleanor slips her shoulder under his arm and puts her own arm around his back. Alice helps guide him from behind. The air is thick with the acrid smell of burning paper and wires, and all three are coughing by the time the circular servants' staircase opens in front of them. The stairwell is largely clear of smoke, but Davy is determined not to make things easy. The stairs swell and ebb as if each step is an ocean wave. Eleanor says, "We'll close our eyes and feel our way down."

"Everything's blurry to me anyway," Franklin admits. "Let me go, Eleanor. I might fall and take you with me."

"No." Eleanor grips him tightly. "We go together."

Alice lets them start down on their own. There's no room for her beside them, and something else holds her back. Other than the people and the snake in her pocket, there is one irreplaceable thing in this house.

The door to the room Teddy shares with Franklin is closed, and when Alice pushes it open, smoke rushes in, greedily expanding its reach.

Her eyes sweep over the detritus of boys' belongings with a sinking feeling. She doesn't see her mother's photograph at first. Holding both hands over her mouth and nose, she forces herself to look again, more slowly this time. And there it is, exactly where Teddy said he'd put it: on the table beside his bed. Alice grabs it and inserts it into the skirt pocket that Emily Spinach is not currently inhabiting. Then she whirls around.

The ghost of Davy Drummond stands in the doorway, crisp and clear despite the smoke billowing into the room.

It's no taller than she, dressed in clothes from the 1850s, with dark hair and a thin, smirking face. Unlike that first glimpse she caught on the evening of the eruption, the ghost appears solid and human. But then, all its illusions seem real until the application of a little reality. Alice charges the door, meaning to pass right through the apparition.

She gets no closer than three feet before colliding with a force that flings her backward so hard, her feet skid. The tail of her spine hits the floor, sending a bolt of pain through her body.

Stay with us, Alice. Voiceless words tickle her ear. *Stay and witness an end to our misery.*

The ghost's image blurs. Suddenly taller, with broad shoulders, it stares at her through the eyes of a young man in his twenties. Another flicker, and it's a girl in her late teens, thin and scared-looking. Alice blinks. The changes come so fast, she can barely catch them all. Another girl, at least two more boys, a man in the prime of his life. She's seeing all the victims of Mrs. Drummond. This thing is like the rat king Teddy wrote about, a terrifying tangle of murderous vermin.

Or, if Mr. Tesla is right, she's seeing the memories imprinted on a house of horrors. *But it's Mr. Edison who is right,* Alice thinks dizzily, struggling to get her legs underneath her. The origin of the ghost is irrelevant when it's trying to kill her. This ghost doesn't even have to wrap icy fingers around her throat to strangle the life out of her. It only has to keep her here, and the smoke will do the job.

The poison in the air thickens, cloaking Franklin's and Teddy's scattered debris. Alice feels more alone than she's ever been as coughs rack her body. She wrenches open the collar of her dress, as if that can help.

Breathe in deeply, Alice. It will soon be over. Your mother's last desire accomplished.

The ghost's taunts open wounds that haven't had time to scab over, let alone heal. There's no point in fighting. Davy will never let her out of this room. She's going to die here.

A vision in scarlet velvet sweeps into the doorway. There's a flash of flying white crystals, floating down over Alice like ash, and then something wet and heavy smacks her full in the face.

"Breathe through that!"

The surprise—and the moisture—rejuvenates Alice enough to press the towel against her face. A strong hand grasps her arm and hauls her to her feet.

"Don't get any of that in your mouth," Eleanor says, her voice muffled.

Get any of what in my mouth? Alice lowers the towel enough to peek above it. Eleanor has dispersed the ghost by showering it with salt, the way Helen did in the Roosevelt house.

They escape into the hallway. As Alice's senses return, she sees that Eleanor has a towel wrapped around her own face, her eyes red and tearing above it. She drags Alice with one hand, and in her other, she carries the box of salt. When Davy Drummond flickers back together in the flame-filled hallway, once more blocking their path, Eleanor throws the whole box at it.

There's nothing left inside. The empty box lands on the floor at the feet of the ghost. Nevertheless, the apparition jumps backward in its unnatural, flickering fashion.

The box is red, with large black letters printed across the front.

It's not salt, Alice realizes with surprise. It's rat poison. *That's* what Alice isn't supposed to get into her mouth. Eleanor has been holding off Davy's ghost with the poison that killed him.

Which gives Alice an idea.

"Drink your tea!" she croaks.

For the first time, the ghost's expression changes. The smirk vanishes.

"Drink your tea, Davy Drummond!" Alice repeats. "Drink your tea for your mama!" The ghost flickers backward, growing more transparent as if hiding in the smoke.

Alice's heart clenches. Taunting Davy with the instrument of his death is too cruel to bear. Davy Drummond was an innocent victim, a child Teddy's age. *But this isn't that boy. Just like that thing in my grandmother's house wasn't my mother.*

With grim determination, Alice drags Eleanor forward, toward the ghost and the servants' staircase. "You lied about my mother. My mother *loved* me, but yours put you in the dirt for thirty dollars!" Her foot bumps the box of rat poison, and she kicks it straight into the center of the apparition.

The creature flies apart like fireworks, disintegrating into sparks of dwindling light. Alice and Eleanor run to the stairs, which are now as clogged with smoke as the rest of the second floor. Clinging to each other, they feel their way down. Just when Alice thinks they're free, the stairwell floods with cold. A shove in the center of her back sends her pitching forward.

She slams into Eleanor, who loses her feet. Together they tumble. Alice's head hits the wall, then her elbow, followed by her shoulder. The soft landing that she ultimately makes is due to her falling on Eleanor, who grunts dully at the impact. The two of them lie at the foot of the stairs, too stunned to move, coughing weakly.

Alice blinks, tears blurring her eyes. In spite of the fire above, frost spreads rapidly down the walls of the stairwell. Davy Drummond is coming to finish them off.

Hands grab her. Lift her.

Someone dumps her on the floor of the kitchen and rolls her over and over while she protests in small squeaks.

Voices break through the spinning fog in her head. Teddy. George. Other boys from the party.

"Get her outside!"

"Her dress is still smoldering!"

"Dump her in the snow, then."

"Have you got Eleanor?"

Hefted into the air again, Alice reflects briefly on the indignity that—after her unkind words about Franklin—*she* is the one carted into the rapturously fresh night like a sack of potatoes.

HOUSE OF FORMER POLICE COMMISSIONER'S SISTER GUTTED

MISDIAGNOSED VENGEFUL BLAMED FOR ELECTRICAL FIRE

MAYOR DEMANDS INQUIRY

New York City, February 25, 1898—The fire department was called last night to the 100 block of East 21st Street, where the home of Mrs. William Cowles, née Anna Roosevelt, sister of former police commissioner Theodore Roosevelt, Jr., was engulfed by flames.

The fire, at first attributed to faulty electrical wiring, has now come under suspicion of supernatural agency. Reports by witnesses claim that the fire began after physical manifestations of a ghost that had previously been diagnosed as Friendly. Mrs. Robert Seaman, better known as the intrepid ex-journalist Nellie Bly, reports that complaints had been made to the Supernatural Registry board about the ghost manifesting behaviors not consistent with that of a Friendly. "I consulted with supernatural expert and inventor Mr. Nikola Tesla, who, after examining the haunting with equipment of his own devising, agreed with me that the more likely designation for this specter was Vengeful."

MAYOR VAN WYCK

Upon hearing of the incident, Mayor Van Wyck demanded an inquiry. "It is outrageous that, in this day and age, our city guild members cannot properly diagnose a haunting, especially in the home of a distinguished citizen such as Mrs. Cowles, whose family, the Roosevelts, have served New York for decades." When asked how this investigation should proceed now that the house is gutted and the haunting nullified, Mayor Van Wyck had no response.

GUILD DEFENDS ITSELF

Mr. Hampton Grier, senior diagnostician for the Manhattan Ghost Diagnostics Guild, denies vehemently that the haunting in Mrs. Cowles's house was misdiagnosed.

"I oversaw that case myself," he said in a public statement. "I am certain that the ghost was a Friendly and that any electrical fire is the result of shoddy workmanship, not malevolent supernatural agency."

Mrs. Cowles was taken to the hospital, where she remains. Other members of the household were treated for smoke inhalation and minor injuries before being released. Mrs. Cowles's husband, Lieutenant Commander William Cowles, is currently serving in the United States Navy in Cuba.

26

ELEANOR THROUGH THE LOOKING GLASS

EVERYONE was relieved when doctors at Bellevue Hospital determined that Aunt Bye wasn't in labor. And she hadn't been poisoned. Or, at least, she'd taken too little to do her harm. They gave her fluids, and the pains subsided quickly. Because of her "advanced maternal age," however, they decide to keep her for a few days of observation.

"Advanced maternal age," Aunt Bye grumbles when I visit her two days after the fire. "I'm forty-three, not a white-haired granny. Oh, Eleanor, I am so sorry."

"Why are you sorry?" I asked.

"We should have abandoned that house after the eruption. That's what Will wanted to do. I was stubborn, putting a house ahead of everyone's safety."

"But the ghost was supposed to be a Friendly, and there was no way of knowing at first that it wasn't."

Aunt Bye presses her lips together and shakes her head. "The moment I started hearing it whisper to me, I should have known. Looking back, what happened seems like a sort of madness. I can't even remember why I was convinced the baby's safety depended on my staying there. I wish I could go back in time and slap some sense into myself!"

I pat her hand. "Vengefuls attack. That's what makes them Vengefuls. This one just did it differently than most."

Instead of threatening us physically, it attacked us emotionally. There *were* those cups of tea and the sugar, but we'll never know if there was poison in them. What we *do* know is that the ghost preyed on our insecurities. It made me overhear a conversation that I am positive never happened. Alice never told me what it said to her, but I can guess what the subject matter was. *Something* made Helen desperate to host that party, and *something* prompted guests to fight among themselves. I bet the others were affected too, although I haven't asked them.

I wouldn't want to tell them what it did to me.

"Where will you go when the hospital releases you?" I ask. "You're welcome at Grandmother Hall's house."

Aunt Bye laughs outright at that, and I smile, happy to have my aunt back to her normal self. "It's kind of you to offer! No, I'll be going to Theodore's house on Oyster Bay and taking Alice and Teddy with me. Edith and the other children will meet me there." She hesitates before going on. "Theodore has resigned his post with the navy to join the U.S. Volunteer Cavalry."

"He's going to war."

"If it comes to that."

I only have to skim the newspaper headlines to know it's coming to that. My heart breaks for Alice.

"Eleanor," my aunt says. "I want to talk to you about something. It's been on my mind for some time, but I wasn't sure . . . not until these past weeks when you've grown so strong. You've been a rock for us to lean on during this difficult time."

My cheeks burn. No one has ever said anything like that about me. It's what people say about Aunt Bye and Uncle Theodore. My instinct is to deny it, to point out every mistake I made. Such as not telling her about the meeting with Nellie Bly, and not making sure Alice was right behind us when I guided Franklin down the stairs.

Then Aunt Bye begins to talk, and I'm riveted by what she has to say.

By the time I leave the hospital room, she's given me a lot to think about. I don't hurry finding my way out to the street where the hired cab is waiting, in spite of Grandmother telling me to make my visit short. She begrudges every penny of this fare, but at the moment, I don't care about her displeasure.

There is money for me to attend the school in London.

Not Grandmother's money, and not Aunt Bye's money either, which Grandmother would label *charity*. Money that belongs to me.

After my grandmother Martha Roosevelt died, her

children each received an inheritance. However, when Aunt Bye and Uncle Theodore were forced to put my father into a sanitarium because of his drinking, they took control of his share, and Uncle Theodore started trust funds for me and my brothers. It is that money that is currently paying for Gracie's boarding school, even though Grandmother led me to believe that *she* was paying for it.

"Your grandmother is your legal guardian, so Theodore and I have been hesitant to interfere," Aunt Bye explained. "I believe it's time for you to make up your own mind. Your grandmother is a lonely woman, but that doesn't give her the right to steal your future."

I gaze out the window during the cab ride home. Ever since the ghost eruption, my life has felt like a surreal version of itself. It's as if I've fallen down a rabbit hole or stepped through a mirror, like the heroine in Lewis Carroll's books, and came out as a different person on the opposite side.

I'm not going to ask Grandmother if I can go away to school.

I'm going to *tell* her.

Not today, though. She told me this morning that she was "exhausted" from having "all these people" in her house. She means Alice and Teddy. I'll wait until they're gone, perhaps a day or two extra for her to recover. Then I'll break the news.

When I arrive home, Grandmother calls out to me from the parlor. "It's about time, Eleanor. You have a guest, and your absence has been holding him up, as well as requiring me to do your duty as hostess."

Poking my head into the parlor, I find Franklin sitting with my grandmother, a tray of tea and a couple of biscuits between them. "Oh, I *am* sorry!" I say to Franklin.

His lips twitch in a smile because he knows what I'm really apologizing for. "I haven't been waiting long." He rises as I enter the room, gives me a cousinly peck on the cheek, and then—before I can cross to another chair—takes my hand and makes me sit beside him.

"How is your head?" I ask.

"Hard as ever," he replies cheerfully. "I'm afraid I've come to say goodbye. I'm taking the train back to Hyde Park late this afternoon."

Since the fire, Franklin has been staying with a relative of his mother's. Helen went home yesterday, as did Corinne. I was happy that Franklin lingered longer.

"I wanted to stay until the end of the week, but Mother insists I come home," he says.

"As well she should," Grandmother declares.

Franklin looks down at his feet. "Considering the situation in Cuba, a summer gathering on Oyster Bay seems unlikely, so I probably won't see you again until Christmas. I was wondering if I may—if you would mind if—I wrote to you?" Slowly, he raises his eyes back to mine.

I'm about to say that of course he may write me and why wouldn't he, when I see the flush in his cheeks. He's not asking to write me as a *cousin*. Once again I feel like Alice. Alice in Wonderland, that is. Not Cousin Alice. "I would like that," I say, the heat rising in my own face.

Grandmother sips her tea, oblivious to the earthshaking change that has occurred.

We talk a little longer, grinning foolishly the whole time, and he stands up to take his leave just as Alice and Teddy return with an avalanche of packages. They've been shopping to replace their things that burned up in the fire. Aunt Edith wired money, and Maisie was recruited to accompany them in the absence of Aunt Bye. There's a great commotion in the foyer as Franklin takes his leave and Grandmother tuts at the wasteful expenditure when "all they really needed was one practical outfit each."

Alice and I escape with her packages, which promptly explode in a hurricane of color and fabric all over my room. "What are you doing?" I ask as Alice digs into the boxes and throws items over her shoulder like a dog digging in a garden.

"Here they are!" Alice holds up a pair of rose-colored silk stockings. "And these." The next pair is ivory and embroidered with colorful hummingbirds. "These are for you," she says proudly, holding them out to me. "Throw out those black ones!"

"I told you not to!"

"When do I ever do what I'm told? You saved my life, Eleanor. That has to be worth two pairs of stockings!" Only Alice could act indignant while presenting a gift.

Hesitantly, I accept them. They *are* beautiful, but . . .

"Why are they so pretty if no one is supposed to see them?"

"Well, *you* see them, silly. Besides, everyone will see them if you wear them with that skirt." I blush, looking down at my midcalf hem, while Alice snaps her fingers and rummages in another bag. "That reminds me. I bought you a new skirt of the proper length. If your grandmother complains, tell her it was made for me but didn't fit."

"I'm supposed to tell her the seamstress accidentally cut it six inches too long?"

"Eleanor, coming back into that house for me was the bravest thing I've ever seen. I don't know if *I* could have done it. If you can't stand up to your grandmother over a skirt, then heaven help you!"

I *can* stand up to my grandmother. A gift is not charity, no matter what she says. Then Alice's words sink in. "Are you saying you wouldn't have come back for *me*?" From the floor, amid the boxes and the wrapping paper, my cousin looks up at me sheepishly. I burst out laughing. "I don't believe that for a second!"

Alice thinks it over. "All right," she admits, "I would have come back for you. But I don't believe I would've thought of bringing the wet towels or the rat poison. I would've charged upstairs with no plan at all, and we both would've been killed."

"That's strange, because I was terrified to go back into the house. But when I did, I thought, *What would Alice do?* And then I knew exactly what to do and in what order."

Her lips spread into a wide grin, and at that moment, I

would tell her my news about school (and maybe even con-fide to her about Franklin) except that Grandmother bellows up the stairs, "Al—ice! You have a visitor!" That's followed by her grumbled comment, which is audible even from a floor below. "Since when did my house become Grand Central Depot?"

27

ALICE, HER FATHER, AND THE REST OF THE TRUTH

HE'S waiting in Mrs. Hall's gloomy parlor—pacing, which doesn't surprise Alice. Her father never stays still for long.

Alice switches on the gas lamps, even though it's against Mrs. Hall's rules. Her father turns to face her when the lights go up. Silent for a long moment, he finally says, "Come here so I can get a good look at you."

Alice's father isn't a tall man, but he is a huge, commanding presence, filling any space he occupies. Alice feels small as she approaches and stands before him.

Clasping his hands behind his back, Father looks her up and down through his spectacles like a general inspecting the troops. "I was told you were not injured. Is that true?"

Well, she coughed up soot for two days and is still black and blue from her tumble down the stairs. "Yes. That's true."

He recommences pacing. "I blame myself. I should have summoned you back to Washington when I first heard about the eruption. Or I should have *insisted* my sister vacate the premises, especially after her husband was called away. As for those incompetent diagnosticians, they should be disbarred and held to account."

"I don't think it was their fault," Alice pipes up. "Mr. Tesla believes this was a rare type of Vengeful and very difficult to identify."

Father adjusts his spectacles. "Who is Mr. Tesla, pray tell?"

"An inventor."

"Never heard of him."

"Well, Nellie Bly thinks highly of him."

Father clears his throat and makes a point of examining a portrait of Mrs. Hall's deceased husband hanging on the parlor wall. "I was also told that you could have left the house safely with your cousins but instead delayed to retrieve a photograph."

Safely is a relative term, as she recalls Eleanor's escape with the stunned and bleeding Franklin, but Alice nods. "It's the only one I have."

Her father stares at the portrait for several more seconds. Then he turns, crosses to the sofa, and folds himself into a sitting position. Removing his spectacles, he lets them hang by their chain and pinches the bridge of his nose.

He wasn't interested in that painting, Alice realizes. He's just having a hard time looking at *her*. Stubbornly, Alice goes to the chair opposite her father and plants herself in it, willing him to face her.

"That is my fault," he says finally.

It takes Alice a second to track that assertion back to her last statement: *It's the only one I have.*

"What has Bye told you about her death?" he asks.

Alice clenches her hands. "I want *you* to tell me what happened."

He raises his eyes to her at last. "You're not going to make this easy for me, are you?"

"Why should I?" Alice feels a jolt of unexpected power over her father.

He laughs shortly, without humor, and looks down at his hands. Alice waits him out, and after twenty or thirty seconds, he begins to speak.

"I was in Albany when you were born, attending to business in the State Assembly. You weren't supposed to come yet, and I thought I would be back in New York City in time. But a telegram arrived, informing me that you had been born early and urging me to return at once. Your mother was very sick with a disease no one knew she had."

Your mother. He has never said those two words to Alice before, unless it was in reference to Mother Edith. Alice shivers and hugs her elbows close to her sides.

"I arrived barely in time." His voice is heavy and almost expressionless, but one of his knees jiggles up and down. "We had no more than a few hours together before she ... before the light went out of my life."

The finality of that statement smacks Alice in the face. For the first time she imagines what her stepmother must feel. To *not* be the light of her husband's life.

"Two days later . . ." Father pauses and busies himself cleaning his spectacles with a bit of cloth. "I did not sleep in those days, and then—*that* night—I went down like a felled tree. Slept for hours and woke suddenly for no reason I understood. I got up and walked into the nursery. And there she was.

"I thought I was dreaming. Or that I had dreamed her death and this was reality. I stood in the doorway like a big, stupid ox, and she smiled at me. I thought everything would be right again." His eyes are shiny, and he does not look at Alice.

"Bye pushed past me into the nursery and yanked the crib away from . . . Because she was holding a pillow over your face. While she was smiling at me, she was trying to suffocate you. I didn't even notice. I was looking only at her. The . . . ghost . . . knocked Bye to the floor, but Bye sheltered you. I stepped in finally, blocking her, trying to reason with . . . her . . . it . . . while Bye escaped with you. She yelled at me to get Mother, and I did, but she was already dead. Mother had been smothered before any of us awoke. . . . I carried her out, but—"

Alice has never seen her father at a loss for words like this, and she doesn't like it. It's as if the ground has changed places with the sky, or a mountain has crumbled into dust. She wants to take back her demand for him to tell her this story. But she's frozen, unable to speak or interrupt, just the way he was frozen in the doorway of her nursery so many years ago.

"I failed Mother, and I failed you," Father says. "If it hadn't been for Bye, we would have lost you. Every single day I remember how I failed my family in their moment of need. But I see that by fixating on my lapse of judgment then, I have continued to fail you in all the days since."

Now Alice is going to cry. She looks away, blinking furiously.

Her father replaces his spectacles. "The house must come down," he says to his shoes. Then he repeats the statement, as if he needs to hear it again. "The house must come down. Bye is right. She always is. It should have come down years ago. When I heard that you and Teddy went in there—"

"It's not her," Alice says quietly.

"What?"

"It's not her. If that's why you kept the house . . ."

"I know that ghost is not your mother," he says gruffly.

But he doesn't deny that her ghost is why he kept the house.

"I'll hire the best extraction crew in the city to retrieve your mother's belongings before the house is razed. Her jewelry. Some favorite belongings. I don't ever want you to think that a photograph is worth risking your life for. There are others, I assure you."

Photographs Alice has never seen. Jewelry. Things he kept from her. Resentment and eagerness seesaw within her.

"I am going to do better, Alice." He says her name slowly and deliberately.

Well, that's a start.

The mantel clock ticks loudly while they sit in silence. Alice is aware of how much it cost her father to tell that story. Although she wishes he had told her the truth long ago, she realizes that she might not have *understood* it without having been in that nursery herself.

When he starts to shift in his seat as if getting ready to stand, Alice blurts out, "Are you going to war?"

Her father nods slowly. "President McKinley has called for volunteers, and it's my duty to answer. I'll be joining the First U.S. Cavalry as second-in-command. We'll be Rough Riders, of a sort." Father offers her a smile. "You remember?"

Alice tries to smile back. "Buffalo Bill's Wild West and Congress of Rough Riders of the World Show. I remember." She was seven years old when her father took her to see Buffalo Bill's famous show. She left determined to become a sharpshooter like Annie Oakley.

Impulsively, Alice launches herself out of her chair and flings her arms around her father's neck. He smells of sandalwood, as always. "You have to come back."

He wraps his big arms around her. "Of course I'll come back."

He sounds confident, and why wouldn't he be? Her father has succeeded in everything he has ever endeavored to do: serving as state assemblyman, running a ranch in North

Dakota, and routing corruption out of the New York City police department.

After those professional successes, the failures in his personal life must haunt him like ghosts that will never fade. The wife who died, the mother he did not save, the brother he could not redeem from drink.

Those ghosts, Alice realizes, are what drives her father to keep moving, to keep climbing and achieving. When he returns from this war—and he *will* return—he won't rest on those laurels. He will pursue something even more exciting.

Alice makes up her mind to support whatever her father chooses next, whether it's another ranch in the Dakotas or the presidency of the United States itself.

And why not the presidency, now that Alice thinks about it?

She'll have to suggest it to him.

May 18, 1898

Dearest Alice,

It is arranged! I will be starting at the Allenswood Academy in London next year. I am so very excited and also terrified. Please tell me everything will be quite all right. I might believe it if it comes from you. I worry about fitting in with the other girls, afraid they will think me strange and awkward. But I remember what you told me, that no one can make me feel inferior without my permission. (I don't remember your exact words, but it was something like that.) I intend to follow your advice as best I can.

Something else has happened. Yesterday, I received an invitation to attend a lecture given by Mr. Tesla on "Questioning the Nature of Hauntings." <u>Guess</u> who invited me! Nellie Bly! She sent two tickets, one for me and one for Grandmother. Grandmother won't go, of course, but she can't forbid me to go because I was invited as Miss Bly's personal guest. I do wish you were here to take the extra ticket, but rest assured I will memorize everything Mr. Tesla has to say and tell you all about it when I next see you.

Speaking of which, Gracie will be home from school in a week, and then, come June, we will join you at Oyster Bay. I cannot wait to see Aunt Bye and our littlest cousin, Baby Will.

As for your idea of running your father for President, I heartily approve! I mentioned it to Franklin in my last letter, and he replied by return post that he thought it was an excellent idea. He says he will support your father for President if you will in turn promise to support him, should he ever choose to run. Can you imagine it? But stranger things have happened, I suppose!

I cannot wait to see you this summer and am counting the days.

With love from your devoted cousin and alter ego,

Eleanor

AUTHOR'S NOTE

This is a work of historical fiction, which means that some of it is grounded in history and other parts are purely invented.

The ghosts are the fictional part. Obviously. So, what's true?

Eleanor Roosevelt was orphaned before the age of ten after her mother and brother died of diphtheria and her father died as a result of his alcoholism. She and her youngest brother, Gracie, were left in the care of their oppressive maternal grandmother, Mary Ludlow Hall. For her own purposes, Mrs. Hall sought to separate Eleanor from her Roosevelt relatives, although Eleanor was permitted to attend their biannual reunions. Eleanor described herself as socially awkward growing up, uncomfortable with peers her own age, and unfashionably dressed. She was self-conscious about her appearance, having been told by her mother at a young age that she was "plain" and "an ugly duckling."

Eleanor's aunt Bye arranged for her to attend the Allenswood Academy in London, which Eleanor later described as having a monumental influence on her life. By the time she was eighteen, a serious romance had developed between Eleanor and her fifth cousin once removed, Franklin Delano Roosevelt. They married in 1905. Franklin would go on to become the only four-term American president, while Eleanor is generally acknowledged as America's most beloved First Lady, known for her political and social work.

Alice Roosevelt was born a few months before her cousin Eleanor. Her mother died of Bright's disease after her birth, and her paternal grandmother succumbed to typhoid fever the same day. Her grieving father relinquished Alice to the care of his sister, Anna "Bye" Roosevelt, but reclaimed her after marrying his childhood sweetheart, Edith Carow. Alice grew up within the Roosevelt household but never quite felt herself a full member of it. Her stepmother was cold, and her father avoided calling her by her given name for most of her childhood. Perhaps for this reason, she developed a rebellious personality and was called, by various relatives, a "wild animal," a "guttersnipe," and a "hellion." In February of 1898, her parents again sent her to her aunt Bye in New York City to separate her from a gang of boys in Washington, D.C., with whom she was "running riot."

When Theodore Roosevelt became president in 1901, Alice catapulted into fame as America's favorite First Daughter. Her favorite color, described as Alice Blue, became the most fashionable color in the United States, and her scandals delighted the press—smoking, driving motorcars, gambling, and carrying around a snake named Emily Spinach. Her father famously stated: "I can either run the country or I can attend to Alice. I cannot possibly do both."

The Roosevelt cousins depicted in this book are real, and there were a good many more I left out of the story because there was no room to fit them in!

If you want to learn more about the Roosevelt family—or about the other historical figures in this story, such as Nellie Bly and Nikola Tesla (who really did build a spirit radio)—check out the titles at the end of this book.

ACKNOWLEDGMENTS

In the spring of 2018, I was "haunted" by an idea about a world where ghosts are real and categorized into three types, but I lacked a protagonist to bring life to an actual story. During a late-night descent into the rabbit hole of Twitter, I stumbled across an article describing the most outrageous First Daughter in American history. I already knew a few things about Alice Roosevelt before reading that post, but I knew a lot more about her famous first cousin by virtue of having taught a biography of Eleanor Roosevelt to fifth-grade students several years earlier. That night I knew I'd found not one main character, but two.

Despite the discovery of a pair of protagonists, this book would never have existed without the support of my agent, Sara Crowe, who believes in me even when I don't believe in myself, and my editor, Sally Morgridge, who saw potential in my weird alternate history and two resilient Roosevelt girls. I also want to thank my excellent copyeditor, Barbara Perris, and the editorial and design teams at Holiday House who created the interior and exterior of this book.

Early on the path toward bookhood, critique partners and beta readers offered invaluable feedback on the story and character arcs. Thank you, Marcy Hatch, Krystalyn Drown, Christine Danek, Jennifer Williams, Maria Mainaro, Pj McIlvaine, Colleen Rowan Kosinski, Darlene Beck Jacobsen, and Kimberly Yavorski for your insight.

Thanks also to my family for cheering me on and for pretending not to mind all the Roosevelt trivia I casually dropped into conversation for months on end.

Finally, I want to express my deep gratitude to the one person whose unwavering support has uplifted me even in the most discouraging times—my best friend, the love of my life and husband, Bob. XOXO forever.

WHAT TO READ NEXT

Burgan, Michael and Hoare, Jerry (illus.). *Who Was Theodore Roosevelt?* Penguin Workshop, 2014.

Christensen, Bonnie. *The Daring Nellie Bly: America's Star Reporter.* Knopf Books for Young Readers, 2003.

Freedman, Russell. *Eleanor Roosevelt: A Life of Discovery.* Clarion Books, 1997.

Frith, Margaret and O'Brien, John (illus.). *Who Was Franklin Roosevelt?* Penguin Workshop, 2010.

Gigliotti, Jim and Hinderliter, John (illus.). *Who Was Nikola Tesla?* Penguin Workshop, 2018.

Harness, Cheryl. *Franklin & Eleanor.* Dutton Juvenile, 2004.

Kerley, Barbara and Fotheringham, Edwin (illus.).*What to Do About Alice?: How Alice Roosevelt Broke the Rules, Charmed the World, and Drove Her Father Teddy Crazy!* Scholastic Press, 2008.

Knapp Sawyer, Kem. *Eleanor Roosevelt: A Photographic Story of a Life.* DK Children, 2006.

Macy, Sue. *Bylines: A Photobiography of Nellie Bly.* National Geographic Children's Books, 2009.

Rose, Caroline Starr and Bye, Alexandra (illus.). *A Race Around the World: The True Story of Nellie Bly and Elisabeth Bisland.* Albert Whitman & Company, 2019.

Thompson, Gare and Wolf, Elizabeth (illus.). *Who Was Eleanor Roosevelt?* Penguin Workshop, 2004.